For Rosemarie —
May Mary be with you,
Edward [signature]

T5-AFC-889

You have not chosen me; I have
chosen you. Go and bear fruit
that will last.

John 15:16

Also available from
Crimson Blue Publishing --

SuperSmart Systems: 5 Simple,
No-Nonsense Steps To Superiority In
Reading Speed, Writing, Math & Memory

by Dr. Edward F. Droge, Jr.

(1994)

THE
MIRACLES

A Novel

Edward F. Droge, Jr.

Crimson Blue Publishing
Greenwich, NY 12834

THE MIRACLES. Copyright © 1995 by
Edward F. Droge, Jr.

Printed and bound in the United States of America. All rights
reserved. No portion of this book may be reproduced in any
form without permission in writing from the copyright owner.
A reviewer, however, may quote brief passages in a review.

Published by Crimson Blue Publishing, P.O. Box 205,
Greenwich, NY 12834

Cover Illustration by Mary Adams Droge

ISBN 0-9637771-2-2

00 99 98 97 96 95   10 9 8 7 6 5 4 3 2 1

for Abigail

for Mary

for the Mother of All Children

ABOUT THE AUTHOR

Edward F. Droge, Jr. earned his bachelor's degree in English from Yale University and both his master's and doctorate in Education from Harvard University, where he taught writing. He is actively involved in his church, and currently he is enrolled in a Formation for Ministry Program.

THE MIRACLES

CHAPTER ONE

DAY ONE

They had not spoken since the priest left.

Mary Depaul puttered at the kitchen sink, lost in thought, rinsing the same dish over and over again, until the running tap filled the basin and threatened to overflow. The rising water jogged her back to the present.

She glanced at the clock. Eight-thirty. Father Dunne had been gone only five minutes or so, but it seemed like another lifetime. For the moment, she felt older than her thirty-five years.

She mused. It hadn't been a long visit. In fact, it had been a rather brief visit, rather to-the-point, rather efficient. Even the poor old priest had seemed somewhat ill at ease and hesitant about his message. It was almost as if he, himself, had had difficulty accepting what he

3

was saying. But, then, he had only been the messenger; he had only relayed what he had been told.

She caught a reflection of herself in the glass of the oven door and poked at her tousled brown hair. She sighed as a thought crossed her mind: The good father must think I'm as sloppy as they come.

She considered her appearance: What a sight, she thought. She not only felt older than her thirty-five years, but she knew she also looked older. The sprinkling of gray hairs amidst the dark brown did not help. She knew she had not been taking care of herself lately. She just could not seem to concentrate these days. There was too much else to focus on, too much else that was more important than how she looked.

She took a step back to see more of herself in the reflection. Hmmmm. She vowed right then and there to cut back on the cookies.

She looked into the living room. Her husband, Matthew, sat on the sofa, staring at the television. In the far corner of the room, near the stairs, an undecorated Christmas tree stood neatly in its stand. It would stay undecorated, Mary thought, until Elizabeth was better. It would have no lights or ornaments or tinsel until then. Elizabeth loved to decorate the Christmas tree; she would be terribly disappointed if she were not able to help hang the lights and ornaments, and to toss on the tinsel.

4

THE MIRACLES

Once more Mary looked at the clock.
In her mind's eye she saw a plane in the night's
sky above the Atlantic. The plane must be in
the air by now, she thought. She guessed that
the trip must take at least five hours, maybe six.
She didn't know for sure. But the plane had to
be in the air by now.

She thought again of Elizabeth. A tear
came to her eye. It seemed she could not think
of Elizabeth lately without that tear forming.
She shook her head. It wasn't fair. It just
wasn't fair. Elizabeth was too young; she had
spent barely six years on the good Lord's earth.
It wasn't fair that she would die.

Mary's mind formed the picture of her
daughter as she lay in her bed upstairs, clutching
to life. While once she had been so vibrant, so
animated, so much a little girl, now, for the last
two weeks, she was so still, so quiet, so
separated from life.

Mary relived the moment. Yet one
more time she saw the car cross the double
yellow line and bear down on her. It happened
so quickly. Too quickly to respond. Or at least
that was what she kept telling herself. But there
was always the nagging wonder: could she
have done anything else -- anything else at all --
to avoid the crash? All who had witnessed it
said no, she could not. It was remarkable, they
had said, that she and Elizabeth had even
survived.

But, Mary wondered, had Elizabeth
really survived? Does lying in bed in a coma for

5

two weeks count as survival? Would she ever wake up? And what would Elizabeth think of the visit that was about to occur? If she were conscious, if she were to open her eyes, what would she think of this? Would she be able to comprehend? Would it overwhelm her? She was special, indeed, not like any other child -- Mary was clear on that -- but even Elizabeth might have trouble grasping the significance of what was about to happen.

But, Mary thought, that was moot, wasn't it? The tear, fully formed now, dripped quickly down her cheek, leaving its own little raised tributary, and, ultimately, it caught the corner of her mouth. She tasted the salt.

All Mary wanted was her daughter back. She was honored, indeed, at the impending visit. But she could not take her mind from Elizabeth.

Mary's eyes narrowed ever so slightly. Her mind flashed the salient pieces of the past six years, the pieces that made her know that Elizabeth was different, was special.

For one brief moment, Mary permitted her mind to run away with the notions that had come to her over the years, the notions that she had dismissed at first, that she had been reluctant to share with Matthew. Eventually, though, she had shared them, albeit without grand fanfare, and she was not quite sure that he was as convinced as she was.

6

THE MIRACLES

Standing there in the kitchen, she nodded her head without realizing it. She often nodded her head when lost in thought.

It just could be, she thought, that Elizabeth, were she awake, would not be overwhelmed at the visit. Not at all. It just could be that Elizabeth somehow knew more of this than even Mary or Matthew or Father Dunne.

Mary's mind wandered. She pictured Elizabeth's big brown eyes and cherubic cheeks. She saw her bangs, neatly trimmed across the full breadth of her forehead. What a sweet child, so filled with love and innocence. She was so fond of everyone and so enjoyed her simple days, helping Mommy bake chocolate chip cookies, sculpting with her clay and home-made molding dough, reading her books.

Her books. Everywhere in this small house were books. No room was void of Elizabeth's piles of books. And each pile had meaning. One pile was designated "just read," one "to be re-read," one "to be re-read yet again," and one "to be read for the first time," always the smallest pile, if it existed at all, given the voracious reading appetite of this little girl. If ever there was a child who read as much as Elizabeth, certainly Mary had never known of her.

There was probably nothing, Mary thought, that meant as much to Elizabeth as her books. Except, perhaps, for Fluffy. Mary flashed a picture of Elizabeth cuddling her black and white stuffed cat, often mistaken for a skunk.

Elizabeth took Fluffy with her virtually everywhere she went, and if Fluffy were not actually engaged in the activity that Elizabeth was engaged in, surely she was nearby. At bath time, Fluffy sat on the rug and avoided the water. At dinner, Fluffy sat within reach so that every now and again Elizabeth could pet her reassuredly, almost mechanically. At bed time, Fluffy snuggled up in her comfy spot near the pillow. Some kids had security blankets; some sucked their thumb for years; Elizabeth had a toy cat that looked like a skunk.

Mary's recollections moved to her daughter's sweet brown eyes the day she knocked the vase from the table. Such sorrow in those eyes for such an insignificant accident. But wasn't that characteristic of Elizabeth, she thought, so deeply sensitive to all those around her, so caring, genuinely caring, always hoping that she could do something to help.

Now Mary wished that she could be the one to help.

*   *   *   *   *

Matthew Depaul, his thick black hair drooping into his eyes, sat by himself on the living room sofa. The light from the television danced on his face but he was not watching. He had no idea what show was on. He stared blankly into the carpet and time after time after time he shook his head and uttered softly to himself: "I can't believe this. I just can't believe this is going to happen." At the moment, like his wife, he, too, felt older than his thirty-five years.

He glanced at the undecorated Christmas tree near the staircase. He would be so happy if his little Elizabeth would wake up soon so that she could take charge of the decorating. Six years old, yet she was a four-star general when it came to leading her mother and father in decorating the tree. Matthew smiled at the thought of it.

He looked up, into the kitchen. He could see Mary at the sink. She was glazed in thought. He could not see the tear in her eye.

It occurred to him that she, too, must have been as stunned as he at the news. It struck him only then that they had not even talked about it yet. While she had gravitated toward the kitchen when Father Dunne left, Matthew had gravitated toward his favorite spot on the sofa.

He stood now and padded across the tiny living room to his wife. His belly jiggled slightly as he walked.

"Did I hear him correctly?" he asked.

She turned toward him. His eyes were locked on hers, and now he could see the faint traces of tears.

She recognized the uncertainty in his eyes. She, too, was uncertain, uncertain of why this was happening, uncertain of how she would be able to live through it, uncertain of what this would do to the family.

"I heard what you heard, Matthew," she said. "And I'm having a really difficult time trying to absorb it."

He shook his head and once more he uttered "I just can't believe it." He paused for a quick assessment in his mind. "But it's a blessing..." He paused again. "...isn't it?"

She nodded.

He tried his best to sound upbeat, but it was a challenge. "Elizabeth will be so pleased when she finds out who was here."

He put his head down, as if he were not fully convinced that his little daughter would ever have the chance to find out. Nevertheless, he would not abandon his hope, nor would he speak in any way that did not seek to exude that confidence. He picked up his head. "She'll be so pleased."

Struck with a thought, his eyes widened and his brows jerked up. "There isn't really much time. We've got to be ready."

Mary's eyes widened now also. He had awakened her from the stupor. "Oh my goodness," she squealed. "The place is a mess."

THE MIRACLES

She scrambled past him into the living room and picked up the throw pillows from the floor. It wasn't a big house, not by any means. They felt fortunate to have it, though, since their meager income would never permit them another option. In the family for three generations, and, passing on to them with the death of Mary's mother, this house was a far cry better than the small apartment they had called home before it.

Despite its small size, however, if she wanted it to be neat and spotless, she would have to work quickly to get it done in time. Her eyes scanned the room as she sized up the job: she would have to vacuum, straighten up, get out the furniture wax...there was much to do.

She set the tasks in her mind as she glanced around the room. The coffee table: remove the magazines and newspapers, give it a quick swipe with the dust cloth. Take the blue pillows up to the bedroom -- the blue clashed with the brown of the sofa anyway. The floor: would she have time to run some oil on it? The parquet would look so rich afterward. She would save that job until the end to see if she could fit it in. Needles from the Christmas evergreen lay underneath it on the floor. She would have to vacuum them first.

She glanced toward the kitchen. The dark wood of the cabinets complemented the yellow decor. But all was not neat. Notes and papers stuck out conspicuously from the

11

refrigerator door: Elizabeth had been playing with the magnets two weeks ago and Mary had not disturbed it. She wanted it to be the same for her, if...no, when...she awoke. She chided herself for not being more positive, more optimistic, like Matthew. Neat or not, the notes and papers would stay just as they were. She continued her survey: the dinner dishes, half finished, were piled near the sink; the counter top needed to be wiped.

Would she have enough time to clean up the house the way she wanted it -- and still be able to throw on some decent clothes? She stopped for a brief moment, took a deep breath, and smiled.

Perspective. She needed perspective. Indeed, they were about to be blessed.

CHAPTER TWO

DAY ONE (Continued)

The man in black shifted uncomfortably in his cushioned seat. His white hair -- very thin on top -- framed kind, blue eyes and a gentle face that invited approach.

He looked out the window. Nothing. He could see nothing but the dark of night. He knew that the chilly depths of the Atlantic lay beneath him, but he could see nothing at this hour and at this altitude, not even a cloud.

Losing himself in thought, compassion etched his face. And from compassion, determination. He had to do this, he thought. He had no choice.

In his mind, he revisited his day. It had been unusual right from the start. He could still hear the voice as if it were speaking to him at this very moment, high above the Atlantic, a

13

voice like no other, an unearthly voice, a voice that could not be dismissed nor forgotten. Yet, it was a familiar voice. He knew it. He had heard it before.

This morning, when he had opened his eyes, there, at the foot of his bed, was the source of the voice. The figure was familiar and made him smile.

The rest of the morning had been so stressful, cancelling appointments, waiting for the arrangements to be confirmed to get him across the Atlantic. More than a few of his colleagues must have thought him eccentric -- at best -- for such an instant decision to alter his schedule. The day had been heavily booked with appointments. This was one of the busiest times of the year.

No matter. He would make up for it somehow. He would reschedule all the appointments. This trip could not wait, not even a day, and this trip was more important than any of his appointments. Much more important.

He settled into his chair and closed his kind eyes. It would be a while yet. He was grateful for the time to think and to pray.

CHAPTER THREE

DAY ONE (Continued)

Slices of gusting rain relentlessly swept the length of 77th Street, compromising the light from the usually reliable streetlamps in this middle-of-the-night dark. The block remained visible, though. Tenement after tenement, attached on both sides, ran halfway down the block, until, rather abruptly, they gave way to single-family homes, also attached on both sides.

The lights from the streetlamps were aided by the colorful lights in the windows. Some of the tenement windows and most of the single-family windows were framed with holiday bulbs -- blinking, blinking, blinking, green and red, yellow and blue, casting their hues out to the stoops that jutted from each tenement and to the very small patches of dirt or grass that sat in front of each house.

77th Street. Heart of Bay Ridge, Brooklyn. Nestled in the metaphoric shadows of the bridge connecting Brooklyn and Staten Island, the Verrazano Bridge, the longest suspension bridge in the world, last time anyone measured.

77th Street. Home of the blue collar worker and the white collar worker. Home of the senior citizen and the Yuppie. Home of the German and the Irish and the Italian.

77th Street. Convenient to the city: at rush hour, only a half hour by subway to midtown Manhattan. Convenient to the suburbs: with no traffic, only a half hour via the Belt Parkway to the south shore of Long Island.

Except for the blinking Christmas lights in the windows, not a movement stirred on the street at this hour, in this weather, in this cold rain, in this December wind. Who in Bay Ridge would be daft enough to be out?

Not a movement. Rain and wind and...wait, what was that? Sure enough. Maybe someone was daft after all. A car turned the corner from 5th Avenue and cruised slowly into the block past the tenements.

The two figures inside the car, barely visible through the sheets of rain smashing against the windshield, strained their necks from side to side, gazing hard, as if searching for an address. The colors of the blinking Christmas

THE MIRACLES

lights in the windows splashed in spurts across their faces.

The car moved slowly, slowly. Past the tenements, the car moved slowly, slowly...until it pulled to the curb on the right side, midway into the block.

For an instant the rain slackened and what were once just figures were now discernible as men and the man in the passenger seat took a phone from the dash and placed it to his ear. The driver scanned the street for movement. Nothing.

Another car, this with a police dome atop and police markings on the sides, likewise turned the corner from 5th Avenue and made its way past the tenements through the rain to the middle of the block. Two more figures were in this vehicle. When it came alongside the first car, it stopped.

The passenger side window of the domed car opened as did the driver side window of the car at the curb. The four figures spoke briefly and the windows closed quickly to keep out the cold and the wet, gusting wind.

The police car with the dome backed up the street slowly, back past the tenements, back toward 5th Avenue. When it reached the intersection, it stopped, blocking the way, preventing further traffic penetration into the street. Its blinking red emergency lights went on to keep it visible in the night.

The rain gusted and splashed without offering a hint of relief.

CHAPTER FOUR

DAY ONE (Continued)

A phone rang at the city desk of the newspaper office. Bright fluorescents from the ceiling washed the desks and cubicles that spanned the floor from wall to wall. As newspaper offices went, this was a typical set-up, but a larger-than-average space -- fitting for the larger-than-life city about which it reported.

Randall Prens, one of only two figures in the office at this hour, picked up the phone on the fourth ring. "City desk," he said mechanically, running his fingers through his blonde hair.

Tie loosened from the collar, loafered feet up on the desk, Prens listened with increasing interest and scribbled in his pad. It got good enough at one point to prompt him to remove his feet from the desk and straighten upright in his chair.

"And you have no idea who it is?" he said after a while. He shook his head with disappointment at the response. "Thanks, Charlie," he said. "I appreciate this."

He hung up the phone and padded in his loafers to the nearby glass cubicle. Lettered on the glass near the door was "Henry Weintraub."

Weintraub, a horseshoe of white hair atop his head and Ben Franklin spectacles on the tip of his nose, was engrossed in Page 3 copy for the morning edition. He heard the loafers as they glided on the carpet into his office. He looked up.

"I just got a tip from my contact at NYPD," said Prens. "Some strange stirrings all of a sudden at headquarters: it seems that Inspector McDougal, Brooklyn South Commander, has been called in to duty, not only in the middle of the night, but in the middle of his vacation."

Weintraub leaned back in his chair, his curiosity obviously piqued.

Prens continued: "The Commissioner, himself, is scrambling several units, apparently for a security detail in Brooklyn."

Weintraub raised his brows. "I thought the Commissioner was out of town at that conference?" he said.

"He is...which makes this all the more intriguing. He's calling the shots by phone."

Weintraub's expression said he found this very interesting. "Must be a pretty big deal if they felt it necessary to get hold of him and not rely on the brass in town to take care of it."

Prens nodded.

"Security detail, huh?" said Weintraub.

Prens nodded again.

"Let's find out as much as we can as fast as we can. If it's big enough, I'll call in someone else to work with you."

Prens needed no other signal and with a final nod he was off, out of Weintraub's office and back to his phone. First order of business was to find out who or what needed security, and where exactly in Brooklyn the detail was reporting. His fingers moved furiously on the telephone's touch tone pad.

CHAPTER FIVE

DAY ONE (Continued)

Rain washed against the side of the white house in the middle of 77th Street and splattered off the dark gray rain gear of the three police officers standing in front. A street lamp a few houses away highlighted the downpour in its glow.

The Depaul house was typical Brooklyn vintage, typical Bay Ridge, typical 77th Street -- brick, attached both sides, small yard in the front. Its windows, too, like the windows of the neighboring houses on either side, were framed with colored Christmas lights, but, unlike the neighboring blinkers, these lights were not lit. The police officers stood together near the house's white picket fence.

One of them leaned toward his partners and asked: "So who the heck is coming in this weather and at this hour of the night anyway?"

The pair shrugged. "Got me," said one. He motioned toward the four police radio cars in the street. "But he's got to be big time to get this attention."

"Maybe it's a movie star," said the first, wishfully.

"What would a movie star want with this house in Brooklyn?" said the second.

"For that matter," said the third, "what would any big timer want here?"

"Who lives here?" the first asked.

The others shrugged.

They all looked toward the window of the house, knowing from the lights inside that the people who lived there were awake.

*   *   *   *   *

Mary Depaul straightened the throw pillow on the couch and then tugged her brown skirt down firmly below the knee. Realizing that she had dressed herself all in brown, she wondered if she should change out of her brown sweater into a white blouse.

THE MIRACLES

Matthew came away from the window and joined his wife. "There are cops all over the place out there," he said.

Mary nodded. "The captain who came to the door before said that there would be."

Matthew cracked a smile. "I wonder what Mrs. Mulrooney's going to say when she finds out about all this."

Mary smiled slightly also: "She's probably looking out the window at the cops right now. I'm surprised she hasn't called."

The phone rang and startled them. They looked at each other as if to say "That's probably her."

Matthew picked it up. From the expression he wore, Mary knew immediately that it was not neighbor Mulrooney.

"Yes, this is Matthew Depaul," he said. There was a pause. "Yes, I understand." Another pause. "Thank you."

He hung up.

Mary looked expectantly at him and when he was not fast enough in identifying the caller, she asked who it was.

"That was the captain again," he said, "calling from his car phone. He said he just received word that the car is out of the airport, on to the Belt Parkway, and should be here at any time. He just wanted to let us know."

Mary swallowed hard and stared blankly at the undecorated Christmas tree by the stairs, again taken by what was about to happen. "Wasn't that nice of him to call," she said

23

mechanically, shaking her head, still struggling
to grasp the import of the visit.

CHAPTER SIX

DAY ONE (Continued)

No sirens blared, but red lights swirled atop the first two police vehicles in a line of six that turned from 5th Avenue on to 77th Street through the unrelenting rain. Uniformed police officers -- gray raincoats on, water splashing off the visors of their caps -- walked in pairs on both sides of the street and paused as the cavalcade passed them.

The first three cars pulled up past the white house with the fence, as the fourth car stopped directly in front. The nearby streetlight shone through the driving rain, illuminating the rear door of the car as it swung open.

A man, dressed in black coat, black hat, and black pants, stepped from the vehicle. With no apparent concern for keeping himself dry, he opened an umbrella and held it above the open door.

Another man, taller and bulkier than the first, alighted from the car. He, too, wore black: a long, flowing cape. He wore no hat and the streetlight bounced off his white hair, very thin on top.

With the first man holding the umbrella for his companion, they walked to the door of the white house. Dozens of police officers on the sidewalk and in the vehicles strained to get a good look.

Mary Depaul and Father Dunne, the gray-haired parish priest with glasses, stood at the open door to greet the visitors. Just behind Mary stood Matthew.

The taller man with the cape entered first, and Father Dunne bowed in reverence. "Your Holiness," said Father Dunne.

Mary's face flushed at the magnitude of the moment and her knees began to tremble. She tried to swallow, but could not. It was happening. He was here. Though she had known for several hours that he would be standing in front of her in her own house, she had not been able to prepare herself for the actual moment. Her palms grew clammy.

The Pope looked exactly as she had pictured him, exactly as he had looked on TV and in the magazines and newspapers. Though he seemed a bit taller than she had expected, he was no different in person than his image

THE MIRACLES

appeared in the media. She was taken by the kindness in his blue eyes.

Though they had not prepared it, both Mary and Matthew followed the lead of Father Dunne, bowed, and said, "Welcome, Your Holiness."

As the Pope unclasped his cape, his companion closed the umbrella and assisted in taking the black garment from the broad shoulders on which it rested. Underneath the cape, the Pope wore simple black clothing: shirt, trousers, and a black jacket. Except for the presence that exuded from him that said clearly he was special, his clothes said that he could have been a parish priest. Perhaps, thought Matthew -- with half a chuckle at it -- he had travelled incognito.

The Pope smiled at his hosts. "I'm so grateful for your understanding and your hospitality. That you have opened your home to me is gracious; that you have done so with such little notice humbles me. Gratias tibi ago."

Mary and Matthew smiled back. Mary wanted to say, "Oh, it's our pleasure," but the words would not make their way from her parched throat. Instead, she drank in the moment; she drank in the presence before her, the warm yct knowing blue eyes, the slightly reddened cheeks, the hair white with wisdom and experience; she drank in the presence of the Vicar of Jesus Christ, the leader of the Catholic Church, the most holy shepherd on earth.

It took an awkward moment by the door before Mary recovered enough to motion everyone into the living room. The Pope's assistant held the cape and Matthew opened the nearby hallway closet. Father Dunne hustled not to be in the way.

"What a lovely home," said the Pope as he stepped into the living room and glanced around politely. Looking at the staircase beyond the living room, he said "I like homes with more than one floor, and this Christmas tree is wonderful." He spoke very good English, but some of it was slightly halting and it was apparent that it was not his primary language. He leaned toward the evergreen and inhaled its fragrance.

Mary was grateful for his polite comments. She knew that their home was small and cramped, but it was so good to hear nice things said about it. "We haven't gotten around to decorating it yet."

He nodded in understanding. A framed photo on the table beside the sofa caught his eye. He bent to see it better, reached for it, but paused before he touched it. Looking at Mary, he asked, "May I?"

"Of course," she said.

He brought the photo closer to his face and squinted ever so slightly. His companion was quick to take a pair of glasses from his inside jacket pocket. He handed them to the Pope who put them on.

THE MIRACLES

The Pope studied the photo for a moment. "This is she," he said. It was a statement, not a question. He looked at Mary for confirmation.

"That's Elizabeth, our daughter."

The Pope smiled. "The sparrow with the thunderous voice."

Mary looked uneasy and confused. The Pope sensed it. He motioned to Mary to sit and when she did, he followed.

Matthew joined Mary on the sofa, as the Pope's companion positioned himself near the Christmas tree and Father Dunne stood unobtrusively on the periphery of the room.

"Has anyone told you why I requested this visit?" the Pope asked.

Mary was not confident with her response: "Only that you wanted to meet Elizabeth."

The Pope nodded.

"But," Mary continued, "how you even know of Elizabeth's existence is quite a mystery to us. How would you know of us here in Brooklyn?" She was hunching her shoulders, emphasizing her bewilderment.

The Pope's eyes said he understood. Again he nodded in reassurance.

"Please let me explain why I am here," said the Pope, "and why it was deemed important enough for an immediate visit."

Mary looked relieved at the prospect of hearing it.

"Do you believe in angels?" the Pope asked Mary.

She hesitated. She suspected that her cheeks were turning red. "Yes," she said. "I believe in angels. I'm not so sure they necessarily look the way the artists have depicted them down through the ages, but I believe that God has created angels, yes."

The Pope smiled. "Oh, I would encourage you to trust the artists in this case. While I share your skepticism about artists' rendering of God and heaven and hell, I have come to know that, for the most part, except for too much emphasis on the wings, the masters have done justice to the angels in their representation of them."

He spoke with such authority. Mary would not doubt him.

"You see..." said the Pope. He paused, searching for the right words. "...let us say that I have empirical knowledge that angels, indeed, do exist. You might even go so far as to say that I have been in the presence of God's heavenly creatures." He paused, knowing that the statement would have an effect. Mary, Matthew, and Father Dunne all opened their eyes just a bit wider when he said it. But they dared not interrupt him.

"Not frequently," he said, "but, yes, I have been visited by angels, serving as God's messengers, most recently this morning when I awoke. And it was in that visit that I became aware of your daughter. The sparrow with the thunderous voice, she was called."

He sensed their uneasiness. "I am sorry not to have referred to her by Elizabeth. It is such a lovely name. I only relate the term used by the angel."

They smiled to ease his mind.

"But why?" asked Mary. "Why would you be told of her? Why would it be so important to prompt you to travel half way around the earth to see Elizabeth Depaul?"

The Pope shook his head ever so slightly. "I have learned long ago not to question God's words. The message was quite clear. There is no question that your daughter is a special child and I was directed to come."

Mary and Matthew both shook their heads as well. Truly this was a wondrous occasion.

"Tell me of Elizabeth," said the Pope. "What kind of a child is she?"

"She *is* a special child," said Mary. "We've known this for several years."

"And what do you mean by special?"

Mary wanted to be clear. She did not want this to seem just a mother's boasting. "She's a very bright child. She writes her alphabet well, and she knows her numbers -- she does some math. I read to her all the time and she listens very carefully to my every word. She has a very good vocabulary. More important, though, she knows more than her years should permit her."

The Pope's eyes said he was intensely interested.

Mary went on. "She knows about life beyond that of a six-year-old. Granted, she reads a lot..."

"An awful lot," Matthew added.

"...but," Mary said, "though she looks like a child and plays like a child, she often has the wisdom of an adult. She has a keen understanding of why things happen and why people do some of the things they do. And..." She paused.

It was clear to the Pope that she was weighing her thoughts carefully, deciding whether to say what she was thinking. He smiled at her to make her comfortable.

"...and," she continued, "she has said that she, too, has been visited by angels..." She paused to note the effect, and, as she expected, the Pope's eyes widened a bit at that. But, otherwise, he remained remarkably composed.

It struck Mary at that moment what an amazing event this actually was -- not only that she was speaking with the Holy Father, Himself, but that they were talking about visits from angels as unremarkably as if they were talking about visits from relatives. She blushed at the calm magnitude of it all.

The Pope's smile remained. It said he understood. It said that he was inclined to trust what Mary would say, no matter how odd. But, then, she thought, visits from angels would not

seem odd to one who, himself, has received
them. He waited politely for her to go on.

She began to see the image of her
daughter in her mind's eye. She saw it very
clearly -- Elizabeth lying eyes-closed,
motionless in her bed, Fluffy lying faithfully
alongside. A tear formed in the corner of
Mary's eye.

She looked to the Pope. "Do you know
of her condition?" she asked.

His face turned somber. "Only what I
have been told by my assistants, who learned
when they inquired that she has been in a
terrible accident."

Water was welling more profusely in
Mary's eyes now. Matthew handed her a tissue
and she dabbed gently before a stream of tears
was permitted to streak her cheek.

"Yes," she said, "it was a terrible
accident. She was in the car with me and we
were talking about how difficult it was to drive
safely and how, even if you were the safest
driver in the world, you couldn't always be
completely safe, because you had no control
over other drivers. We were only a few blocks
from here...and another car crossed the double
lines...and..."

The Pope reached his hand across to
touch her gently on the cheek. She was
comforted by the gesture.

"She lost consciousness at the scene and
she hasn't regained it yet. And, now, the

doctors have also been concerned about
pneumonia."
"She has not spoken since the accident?"
asked the Pope.
Mary nodded.
"How long ago was that?" he asked.
"Two weeks now."
The Pope lowered his head as if in
thought, or prayer. He pinched the bridge of his
nose with his hand and closed his eyes
momentarily. He raised his head and said softly,
"May I see her?"
"Of course," said Mary. "She's
upstairs."
They both got up at the same time, and
immediately Matthew did, too. Mary led them
to the staircase. Father Dunne and the Pope's
assistant followed at the rear as they climbed to
the second floor.
Elizabeth's room was softly lit. Shelves
lined the walls and on the shelves were dolls and
stuffed animals of every ilk and flavor. The
walls were papered with a light floral pattern,
bordered in pink, which gently declared itself
the prominent color.
The bed was against the far wall and
Elizabeth lay quietly on her back, eyes closed,
her arm connected by tube to an intravenous
bottle hanging nearby. Her face was pale,
washed with the soft light, but clearly this was a
striking child, with smooth, unblemished cheeks
and light brown hair to her shoulders. Fluffy,

THE MIRACLES

her black and white stuffed cat that resembled a skunk, lay faithfully at her side.

Mary entered the room first, followed by the Pope, and by the time Father Dunne had stepped in, the lack of space was conspicuous. They all stood cramped but quiet for a moment, peering at the lovely little girl that lay so still before them. Once more the water welled in Mary's eyes, and she took the well-used tissue to them immediately.

The Pope moved closer to the bed and Mary moved aside to make room. He lay his hand gently atop the child's and closed his eyes. "Avis," he said. "Vox clamantis in deserto." He stayed in this position and it was as if he was not at all aware of anyone else in the room with him except Elizabeth.

His assistant made a motion to all that, perhaps, it would be better if the Pope were permitted to be with her alone. All understood, and slowly they proceeded from the room and down the stairs.

Back in the living room, Matthew was the perfect host and brought everyone coffee, tea, and soft drinks. Mary sat on the sofa, dazed a bit at first, every few minutes glancing toward the top of the stairs, expecting to see the Pope standing there, ready to descend.

The minutes went by slowly, but before Mary realized it, more than an hour had passed. She decided to check in on them. She rose, excused herself, and took the stairs to the second floor.

Edward F. Droge, Jr.

The Pope was kneeling at the bedside
now, again his one hand pinching his nose, as
his other still lay atop Elizabeth's. Mary was
moved by the sight. She did not understand
fully what was going on, and she knew that she
was going to be overwhelmed by this visit once
she had had a chance to absorb that it was
actually taking place, but for the moment she
was moved and comforted by the Vicar of
Christ at her child's bedside. No one, she
thought, no one would serve as a better
spokesman to God than the gentle man on his
knees a few yards away.

She withdrew slowly and quietly, and
she wondered whether or not the Pope had even
sensed that she was there. She joined the others
downstairs.

Matthew's eyes said that he wanted to
know how it was going up there. "He's still
praying," was all that she said. For all present,
it was all that she needed to say.

Another half hour passed before a
movement at the top of the stairs caught Mary's
eye from the sofa. She looked up to see the
Pope as he began his descent. He looked tired,
she thought, exhausted, in fact. But as she
moved to meet him at the bottom of the
staircase, he smiled at her just the same, as if he
were not the least bit weary from the long trip
and the intense prayer.

"She is a very special child, Elizabeth
is," he said. "She moved not at all and spoke

36

not at all, but it could not be clearer to me: she is a very special child."

Mary did not know what to say except to nod thanks and to smile at the kind words. When he reached the bottom of the stairs, his assistant moved to his side and Mary continued upward to check in on her daughter.

Elizabeth lay as still as ever in her bed, faithful Fluffy at her side. Mary stood staring at her daughter for a moment, staring at the innocent face, staring at the motionless little body, all tucked under the covers, and she asked God ever so fervently to have mercy on her and on her family by bringing her sweet Elizabeth back to them soon. She bent and kissed Elizabeth's forehead and turned the lamp down a notch for softer light.

When she returned to the living room, the Pope was engaged in conversation with Father Dunne on the sofa. With Matthew's help, the Pope's assistant was retrieving his own coat and the Pope's black cape from the closet near the front door.

"Can I get more refreshments?" Mary asked.

The Pope's assistant was polite but quick to respond: "No, thank you. You've been very kind already, but we must be going."

Father Dunne rose to give Mary the space on the sofa. She sat and the Pope smiled at her with his eyes.

"I'm so grateful for your visit," she said. "And for your prayers."

"You are gracious for allowing me the privilege of coming to your home -- in the middle of the night, with very little notice. I am humbled. Thank you."

She blushed a bit at his humility.

He could see the concern in her eyes.

"Have faith," he said. "God is at work here, you can be sure. That I was directed to you as I was cannot be viewed as anything but divine intervention. Have faith that all will be well."

His words filled her with courage and strength. "I know that if Elizabeth were awake she would thank you herself for coming to see her. This is a blessing that she would never forget."

In a most sincere voice, he responded quickly: "It is I who have been blessed by this visit with Elizabeth. I do hope that she recovers soon and that you will bring her to visit with me again. I know that I would enjoy speaking with her."

Mary was awed at the thought of it, but, of course, agreeable. "I'll let you know as soon as she wakes up. Thank you, Your Holiness."

"I saw the cards by her bed," he said. "Was it her birthday recently?"

"Ten days ago. December 8th. She just turned six."

"December 8th!" He was surprised. "Well, December 8th is a good day to have a birthday."

Mary smiled. "The feast of Our Lady's Immaculate Conception."

THE MIRACLES

He smiled back. "A very special feast day."

She nodded in acknowledgement.

He touched his hand to her forehead and she bowed her head toward him slightly for his blessing. He closed his eyes and offered his blessing softly in another language that Mary guessed to be Latin.

When he finished speaking, he remained silent in prayer for a moment, his eyes still closed, his hand still touching her forehead. She prayed in silence as well.

In a few seconds he opened his eyes, removed his hand, and stood. Immediately, his assistant was at his side with the cape.

They all exchanged pleasantries as the Pope and his assistant made their way out. When the door opened, Mary was pleased that the rain had stopped, making the departure less hurried. It was still cold and dark, and the only light came from the streetlamps and the few blinking holiday bulbs on neighboring homes.

"I will pray for her," said the Pope, and, sweeping his eyes from Mary to Matthew and back to Mary, he added, " and I will pray for you." His eyes said a special farewell to her, and the corners of her mouth turned up ever so slightly in return. A tear fell to her cheek as the Pope stepped out into the night.

"Someone will be in contact with you soon," said the Pope's assistant to Mary and Matthew, before hustling out.

They nodded, not fully comprehending what had just taken place, not yet feeling the full impact of the moment. Their eyes showed clearly the daze of their minds at the whirlwind nature of this incredible visit.

Father Dunne rushed to the door to catch up with the Pope. "I'll call you tomorrow," he said as he left.

Mary looked out into the street. Bay Ridge, Brooklyn -- 77th Street -- had been granted an unusual honor and had not had time to prepare for it. She wondered how many of her neighbors were even awake, how many were even aware that someone very, very special had chosen to visit in the middle of the night. He had come because an angel had told him to come, he had said. Mary shook her head at the mystery and majesty of the moment.

Police officers mulled about near the waiting cars, which were sitting exactly as they had been left. Beads of rain flew from the door of the big black car in front of the house as a uniformed policeman swung it open swiftly for its passengers. With one slight wave, the Pope was in the car, followed by his assistant, and in a moment the door closed and he was gone. The car, escorted by police vehicles, sped away down the street and turned the corner.

Matthew put his arm around Mary and they stood in the doorway, staring blankly at the night for a moment, trying desperately to grasp it all. It had happened so fast; such a momentous occasion, a once-in-a-lifetime

THE MIRACLES

occasion, an occasion that people often dream
of but never fulfill, had been swept upon them
and they were breathless at the honor, and
confused at the significance.

CHAPTER SEVEN

DAY ONE (Continued)

The morning light washed the floor of
Elizabeth's room from the window to the bed.
Mary, half-seated in a chair beside the bed, half-
resting on the mattress, with her head lying at
Elizabeth's side, opened her eyes and wondered
how long she had been asleep. She was not
wearing her watch but guessed that it had been
only an hour or so. It could not have been more
than two hours since the Pope had left, she
thought. As she was accustomed to doing
occasionally, she had stayed with Elizabeth
rather than going to her own bed. She wanted
to be present in the event there was any sign of
her daughter's awakening.

She looked at Elizabeth, lying quietly
before her, motionless, except for the slow
rhythm of her breathing. Mary's heart sank to

see her so still. Fluffy, ever faithful, lay at her daughter's side.

The liquid in the intravenous bottle dripped slowly into the tube that carried it into Elizabeth's arm. Mary noted that the bottle was low. She would have to replace it soon.

Mary squinted at Elizabeth. Something seemed different this morning, she thought, and at first she was not able to discern it. In a moment, though, it became clear: it was Elizabeth's face -- her lips. Mary stood to get a better perspective. Yes, her lips. There was no mistaking that they were slightly curled up at the ends. Elizabeth was smiling. Mary made the sign of the cross and said a quick prayer of thanks. Indeed, Elizabeth was smiling.

This was the first change since the accident, the first movement of any kind that her little girl had made. As slight as it was, it was a movement, and Mary would not be denied the pleasure of it.

Still standing by the bed, she was about to leave to see if Matthew were awake so that she could tell him the wonderful news, when she stopped abruptly and gasped to catch her breath at what she thought she saw. Movement. She thought she saw movement on the bed, near Elizabeth's right hand, which was lying atop the covers. Had it been her imagination?

Mary stood absolutely still and held her breath as she waited for confirmation. Please,

Elizabeth, do it again, she thought. Please, show me that I was not imagining it.

A moment passed. Nothing. Mary controlled her breathing so that it would not interfere with her ability to see even the slightest motion. Another moment passed. And then another. Still nothing.

Mary began to doubt herself. It easily could have been, she thought, the thrill of seeing her daughter's smile that had fooled her into seeing another sign of improvement. She probably had seen only what she had wanted to see.

Yet another moment went by and Elizabeth lay as still as ever, her slow and steady breathing the only movement on the bed. Mary, herself, began to breathe a bit more regularly now, slowly convincing herself that she had been caught up with the joy of the smile, and still relishing in that clear change. There was no doubting that Elizabeth was smiling.

Mary relaxed her body and committed herself once again to checking on Matthew. He should see the smile, she thought. He should see it as soon as possible. Even if he were asleep, she thought, she would wake him. It was too important a development to risk having him not see it as soon as possible.

Mary turned to leave, and suddenly she felt a shiver run down her spine. She turned back to face Elizabeth. Once more she had seen a movement, this time in her daughter's eyes.

THE MIRACLES

The lids had definitely moved. Mary was certain of it. And it was not the routine movement of a REM dream state, where the eyes would dart from side to side or up and down. Mary's many years of nursing, tending at the side of sleeping patients, had made her quite familiar with REM movement, and she was certain that that was not what she had seen. She had seen Elizabeth's eyelids move slightly, almost as if she were about to open them. She knew the look. She was sure of it.

She did not doubt herself this time. Though she had been turning to leave, she was certain that she had seen Elizabeth's eyelids move. Again she held her breath and froze her body in observation and expectation.

She studied her child's face, her bangs cut straight across so neatly, her lips still curled at the ends. Mary raised her thoughts to heaven and prayed for another sign.

Elizabeth's eyelids moved again. Mary had been watching intensely. There was no room for doubt now. None at all. She prayed more vigorously.

Suddenly, as if awakening from a night's sleep, Elizabeth opened her eyelids and her big brown eyes could be seen. Mary dropped to her knees at the side of the bed.

"Mommy?" Elizabeth said softly.

"Yes, dear," Mary said, tears falling from her eyes. "Yes, Elizabeth, Mommy's here." She lay her hand atop Elizabeth's.

Elizabeth looked down to see her mother alongside, and the smile grew bigger. Their eyes met and stayed locked in place, mother and child, each comforted by the presence of the other. Elizabeth caught a glimpse of Fluffy and Mary moved the black and white stuffed cat closer to her daughter's hand. Elizabeth cradled her faithful companion as best she could, despite the intravenous tubing. Rubbing her eye with her other hand, she struggled to get both of her eyes completely open, and she seemed confused.

"It's okay, sweetie," Mary said in a comforting tone. "It's okay." In silence, she thanked God for bringing her little child back to her.

Elizabeth opened her eyes wider now. "Mommy..."

"Yes, dear."

"...Mommy, just before I woke up I had a dream."

"Of what, Elizabeth?"

"I dreamed I was awakened by an angel."

Mary's mouth opened a bit, as did her eyes. She had no doubt that God had listened to her prayers and to the prayers of the Pope. In her mind, she said "Thank you. Oh, God in heaven, thank you." She was crying heavily now. She hugged her little Elizabeth. "Oh, my God, thank you," she repeated in silence, over and over again.

CHAPTER EIGHT

DAY ONE (Continued)

The front bell rang three times before
Matthew was able to answer it. He was
toweling his hair dry when he opened the door.

The morning sun shone brightly over the
visitor's shoulder, making his face difficult to
see. His thick blonde hair, however, was easily
discernible.

"Mr. Depaul?" the visitor asked.

Matthew nodded.

"My name is Randall Prens. I'm a
reporter with the..." He held up a laminated
identification card, but before he could finish his
sentence, Matthew interrupted.

"I've noticed your byline," Matthew
said. "I've read some of your stories."

Prens was obviously surprised by the comment, unaccustomed to anyone recognizing his name.

Matthew was squinting into the sun. He motioned Prens forward. "Please, come in," he said.

Prens nodded gratefully and stepped into the house. Out of the sun, his somewhat disheveled look hinted at his having been up all night, or, perhaps, at best, having caught a few winks at his desk.

"What is it you want?" Matthew asked, remaining by the door as he closed it.

"I'm following up a report we received last night that a VIP visited this neighborhood -- in fact, this house -- in the early morning hours. Is that true?" As best he could, without seeming too much of a snoop, Prens glanced around the house. He noted the undecorated Christmas tree near the stairs.

Matthew was silent. It had not occurred to him until this very moment that the visit would make an interesting news story. But of course it would, he thought. Of course it would. He chided himself for not having thought of it sooner.

Prens smiled and continued: "Did you have a celebrity visitor last night, Mr. Depaul?"

"A celebrity? A V.I.P.? In this house?"

Prens nodded.

Matthew tried to put him off. "That would be unlikely, don't you think?"

Prens tilted his head. "Unlikely? I wouldn't know. But, unlikely or not, did you have such a visitor?"

"Now why would that be of any importance to you or your readers?" Matthew made a concerted effort to speak in a polite tone. He was stalling, searching for the appropriate way to handle this.

"It's news, Mr. Depaul. It's, perhaps, big news, don't you think, if a big celebrity blows into town and gets a police escort to a little house in Bay Ridge? We know for certain that he -- or she -- received a police escort."

"Even if we did have a visitor, I'm not sure it's newsworthy," Matthew said, determining on the spot to protect his family from the disturbance that a news story about the visit would create. He wished he had anticipated this and had given himself more time to think it over, more time to decide how best to handle the inevitable questions from reporters.

"I appreciate your reticence, Mr. Depaul, I really do," said Prens, though he really did not appreciate it, "but I hope you can appreciate my sense of duty to the public...not to mention the expectations of my editor. If I don't come back with some information, I may find myself back on the obit desk." He knew that that would not happen, but he would try anything that he felt could work.

Matthew shrugged, still toweling his hair.

Prens winked. "What if the president visited you in the middle of the night? Or a rock star or a famous actress? Don't you think that's news?"

"But then you'd have a lot of questions for me, wouldn't you? Wanting to know why they visited and how I know them or if I'm related to them. You'd have a lot of questions, probably, that I wouldn't necessarily feel disposed to respond to, since -- it would be my judgment -- I would feel no responsibility to you or to the public to share what happens in the privacy of my home."

Matthew was careful to remain polite. He had no quarrel with Prens. He did, however, feel that he needed more time to think about how to respond to his questions. If, eventually, Matthew determined it best to acknowledge the visit, then he would be very cooperative. Until then, though, he preferred to be evasive.

Prens was persistent. "Even if it's a public figure?" He leaned against the door.

Matthew shook his head. "Especially if it's a public figure."

Prens was smiling, trying ostensibly to take the edge off what could otherwise grow into a tense situation. But his few years of experience had taught him that it does not pay at all to get on the bad side of a news source -- or potential news source. The way this conversation was going, he knew he had come to the right place. His police source had given him the correct address.

But he still did not know who the visitor was, and, until he did, he had no story. The police on the scene had been no help, the driving rain having prevented all present from getting a good look. One cop had thought it was a particular country singer, all dressed in black, but it hadn't taken Prens long to find out that that particular singer had been performing in Branson, Missouri last night, and, besides, Prens had figured, though that singer was a super celebrity, he was hardly the kind who could command such police attention, what with a full escort and all, and the Commissioner calling the shots from out of town. No, it wasn't a country singer. It had to be someone bigger.

He ran his fingers through his blonde hair, pulling it up away from his face. "Mr. Depaul," he said, "I understand what you are saying, I really do, and I want to assure you right now that I will cooperate with you if you help me out here. Just tell me who visited last night, who merited the police escort, and I promise I won't even ask another question. I'll figure out some other way of finding the answers to my remaining questions, without having to bother you any further."

Matthew reached slowly for the doorknob and Prens moved politely to accommodate him. "I appreciate your understanding, Mr. Prens, but I don't have anything else to say. I don't know who pointed you here, but maybe you should go back to him or her and try to get more information." He opened the door and the sun shone in.

"You aren't saying that you had no visitor, are you, Mr. Depaul?"

"I'm only saying that if we did have a visitor, I wouldn't necessarily think it a good idea to share it with the press."

"But you know that sooner or later we'll find out. You're only postponing the inevitable."

Matthew was soft spoken. "It's a pleasure to meet you, Mr. Prens. Good luck to you."

Prens took the hint and stepped slowly out the door, but not without just one last shot: "Was it the president, Mr. Depaul? Just tell me if it was the president?"

Matthew began to close the door and a sparkle came into his eye. "I can tell you in all truth, Mr. Prens, it was not the president. But, I do have a thought..." He hesitated, like a child with the top of the cookie jar in his hand, trying to be certain it was really what he wanted to do.

"Yes," Prens said, putting his hand in his pocket for his pencil. At this point he was thrilled at the prospect of getting some information, any information.

"...What if I said a few words and let you try to figure out what I mean?"

"Sure," said Prens. He would take any hints he could get.

THE MIRACLES

The smirk on Matthew's face could not be denied. He looked Prens in the eyes and said simply: "...I'm not saying it was an angel, but if you printed that, you wouldn't be able to get me to deny it." He was smiling at the simple truth of the statement as he closed the door gently.

CHAPTER NINE

DAY TWO

Mary hummed a Christmas tune as she tended to a pot of coffee at the kitchen counter. The dinner dishes were piled in the sink.

Her mind turned to Elizabeth. It had been only a day now since she had awakened from her coma, but she seemed as sharp as she ever was -- in fact, maybe even sharper. Mary smiled at that. It was so good to have her daughter back again.

Her thoughts drifted to the phone call to the Pope. He had been so pleased and so politely insistent that he meet Elizabeth at the first possible opportunity. With Advent and Christmas, he had a very busy schedule for the next couple of weeks, but he would see if it were possible to stop back in New York after the Christmas season. If she were well enough,

THE MIRACLES

Mary and Matthew could bring her to see him then, even if it were just at the airport.

Mary agreed, thrilled at the prospect of her little one being able to thank the Pontiff in person. She knew that Elizabeth would be delighted at the prospect as well.

"You were very kind to come all that way," Elizabeth had said to him at one point on the phone.

He had appreciated the telephone conversation, but still he looked forward to speaking with her face to face. Mary was confident that they could work it out.

Mary's mind returned to the coffee pot and the kitchen as her little Elizabeth bounded to her side with bare feet. She was cuddling Fluffy in her arms. Elizabeth's bangs, freshly cut in a straight line along the top of her brows, showcased her big brown eyes.

Mary put her hand on her daughter's shoulder. "What's up, sweetie?"

"Daddy said that Aunt Barbara and Uncle Al are coming over."

"That's right. They want to see you and say hello. I'm making some coffee and Daddy brought home a chocolate cake for dessert."

"Mmmmm. Chocolate cake sounds good."

Mary patted her on the head. "You can have the biggest piece."

Elizabeth smiled at that.

"When is Aunt Barbara going to have her baby?" Elizabeth asked.

"In about two months," Mary said. She was struck by the thought of it -- her baby sister, Barbara, was, herself, going to have a baby. She shook her head in awe. It didn't seem all that long ago when Mary was changing Barbara's diapers. Where had the time gone?

"Is she going to have a boy or a girl?" Elizabeth wanted to know.

Well, they're coming here straight from the doctor's office and we may know the answer to that question tonight."

The door bell rang. "You can ask her yourself," Mary said. "That's probably Aunt Barbara and Uncle Al right now."

Mary opened the door and her younger sister stood before her in the evening light, eyes red, tears streaming from them. "Oh, my goodness, Barbara, are you all right?" Mary stepped close to her and put her arm around her to lead her inside. "Where's Al?"

"He's looking for a parking space," said Barbara, her middle swollen with child.

Mary closed the door. "What's wrong, sweetheart?"

She helped her take off her sweater. Barbara was big for seven months.

"I've lost the baby," Barbara said, and saying it made her cry even more heavily now. The smooth skin of her face was very red, as were her eyes. She looked so healthy otherwise, her face a bit round from her having taken on weight with the pregnancy, but her overall appearance remarkably sound for a woman seven months with child.

Mary's mouth dropped at the news. "Lost the baby! But...how can that be?"

"Remember how I mentioned a few times in the past couple of days that it seemed to have been so calm -- no kicking, no pinching, no turning. At first I was glad to have some relief, but after a while, it made me nervous. It seemed too calm."

Mary was nodding in confirmation. "I remember," she said. "I remember."

Barbara could not control her tears but she struggled through them to talk with her sister. "I had this appointment with the doctor scheduled, anyhow, and so I waited until today to bring it up to him. He examined me and gave me an ultra sound and took some tests and..." She had to gather the strength to say it. She grabbed hold of Mary's wrist and tightened her grip. "...he doesn't know the cause yet...but there's no question about the vital signs...oh, Mary..." She couldn't go on, and she did not have to: it was all too clear to Mary, who brought her close to her and squeezed her tightly. Both of them stood near the undecorated Christmas tree, crying, hugging.

Mary did not know what to say. What can anyone say to comfort a mother who loses her child? Mary understood the pain and again thanked God that she had not lost her own child.

Elizabeth had been standing to the side and had heard all. She, too, was crying. She stepped closer to her aunt and outstretched her arms. Her head lay against Barbara's bulging tummy.

Elizabeth listened. Nothing. The last time she had listened at this spot, she had heard life. This time, however, there was no life to hear.

*　　*　　*　　*　　*

Matthew and Al talked solemnly in the kitchen as they washed the dishes, and Mary, Elizabeth, and Barbara sat on the sofa, the former two trying their best to console.

Mary was shaking her head. "...and he was clear that you had to carry the full term? Another two months?"

"He said he would talk to me more about that, but that for now I should be thinking that way. There are serious risks to be considered otherwise, but I was so broken up in his office, we decided it would be better to talk about it again in a day or so."

The men, finished with the dishes, now moved into the living room.

THE MIRACLES

Al, a heavyset man with thick, dark hair, was holding Barbara's sweater. "We should be going," he said.

Mary nodded. She looked at her sister's red eyes. "You must be exhausted."

Barbara's expression said that she was. She struggled to get up and Mary and Elizabeth stepped closer to help.

"Thanks for everything," Barbara said. "I'm glad you were here for me."

Mary hugged her. "I'm always here for you. Please let me know if there's anything I can do."

Barbara nodded and tried unsuccessfully to force a smile. She looked to Elizabeth. "And, you, my little princess. I'm sorry I didn't have a chance to visit with you without all this troubling news to distract us." She held out her hands. "I'm so glad to see you well again."

Elizabeth stepped closer and outstretched her arms. Again she laid her head on her aunt's bulging tummy. This time, however, she closed her eyes and prayed.

Barbara hugged back as best she could, and suddenly her eyes opened wide. Mary noticed it immediately. "What is it?" she asked her sister. "Are you all right?"

Little Elizabeth was still hugging, still with her eyes closed, still praying.

Mary put her hand on Elizabeth's shoulder. "Step back a minute, sweetie. Your Aunt Barbara needs some room."

Again Mary asked her sister if she was all right.

Barbara took a deep breath. "For a moment there I..." She hesitated, trying to find the right words. "...I thought I felt something, as if...as if the baby moved again."

Mary gasped slightly.

But Barbara shook her head. "I'm sorry. I'm sure it was my imagination. I didn't mean to startle you."

Mary did not know what to say, and so she let it go.

They said their good-byes and Al led Barbara down the steps and down the street toward the car. The blinking Christmas lights from the neighboring homes splashed their colors on them in bursts.

Everyone waved, and when it was clear that the pair were safely in the car, Mary waved once more before stepping back into the house.

She leaned against the door and stared blankly for a moment, gathering her thoughts on the visit. She wished that she could have been more of a comfort for her sister, and she was disappointed with herself that she could not think of better things to say.

Her thoughts were broken by catching something out of the corner of her eye. She turned to see Elizabeth, sitting quietly on the sofa, eyes closed, hands together in prayer.

Mary approached.

Elizabeth opened her eyes at her mother's presence.

THE MIRACLES

"What are you praying for, sweetie?"
Mary asked softly.

"For the baby, Mommy. I'm praying for
the baby."

"Is that what you were doing when you
were hugging Aunt Barbara?"

Elizabeth nodded.

CHAPTER TEN

DAY THREE

Mary strolled along the periphery of the park as Elizabeth skipped playfully ahead of her. The crisp December air was kindly tempered by a strong sun. Mary admired the Christmas garlands that were strung along the top of the park fence.

She mused as she walked, thankful for having her daughter back. Truly, she was blessed to have such a special little girl. Life was almost back to normal now, as it was before the accident. Elizabeth's weight was down a bit from having been inactive for so long, but that was coming along nicely. Another week or so of her regular diet, Mary thought, and the weight would return.

They approached the intersection at the edge of the park and Elizabeth waited for her mother to catch up. Mary joined her in a moment and took her hand to wait for the light to turn green.

Nearing noon, traffic was beginning to grow heavier, but the flow seemed routine. The green light for the cross traffic changed to yellow and was about to turn to red when, without warning, in the avenue away from Mary and Elizabeth, a pick-up truck in mid-block accelerated toward the corner, apparently trying to beat the light.

Mary saw the development and pulled Elizabeth close to her. The truck was heading in their direction.

The light changed to red for the cross traffic but the pick-up continued at a fast pace. Meanwhile, the light changed to green for the perpendicular traffic. Several cars -- among them a light blue sedan -- started forward just as the pick-up reached the intersection. Mary backed up and brought Elizabeth with her. She could sense what was about to happen.

The pick-up sped into the intersection and, with a loud, violent whack of metal crashing metal, a sickening, deafening sound of mashing and clashing and smashing, it slammed into the side of the blue car. The collision was of such force that it sent the blue sedan reeling sidewards recklessly in the direction of Mary and Elizabeth and when it reached the concrete island in the center of the avenue, it rolled over -- once, twice, three times it rolled over, faster and faster, at a violent speed, tearing the door from the passenger side, throwing a passenger out of the vehicle. Finally, mercifully, it heaved in the air about fifteen feet from Mary and Elizabeth and crashed to a halt on its side in the street.

Mary and Elizabeth watched in shock. They were so close. Mary had frozen in place and had been unable to move away quickly. She blessed herself and thanked God that they had been spared.

The mother and daughter in the sedan had not been so lucky. Mary could see now that the passenger that had been thrown from the vehicle was a little girl, lying face up, appearing to be six or seven years old. She had landed in the street not more than ten feet from Mary and Elizabeth.

Mary rushed to her side. The child was not breathing. Mary touched her throat. No pulse. She leaned her ear to her chest. Her years of medical training, nursing in emergency situations, told her immediately that the little girl was dead, beyond help from CPR or from anything else Mary could do for her. Her attention now turned to the girl's mother who was still in the car.

All traffic stopped. Passersby and people from the stopped cars ran to the blue sedan. It was on its side. Mary was the first to reach it and immediately she climbed to the woman at the steering wheel. She was strapped in with her seat belt and was suspended, the weight of her body pulling her downward. She appeared to be unconscious, but, Mary thought, at least she was alive.

Elizabeth walked slowly toward the motionless body of the little girl lying in the street. All attention of the others was on the woman in the car.

Lying near the girl's body was a teddy bear. Elizabeth picked it up and brought it to the side of the girl.

Elizabeth stood quietly for a moment, staring at the body before her, a girl not much older than she, lifeless, crumpled in a heap, the air biting at her deathly pale face.

Elizabeth knelt beside her. She placed the teddy bear in the little girl's arms.

Putting her hands together, and her head down, Elizabeth began to pray. She prayed to the Blessed Virgin Mary.

"Dear Mary, Mother of Jesus, please pray for this little girl. You know what it is like to have a child. You know how this little girl's mother will feel when she finds out that her daughter has been killed. Please ask your son, Jesus, to have mercy on them both."

She stayed like that in prayer near the little girl's body as a growing number of people worked to free the mother from the sedan. Neither the noise at the scene, nor the sirens in the distance growing closer with each passing moment, deterred Elizabeth from her vigil.

Mary had been successful in speaking with the woman in the car, comforting her, telling her that she would be all right. The ambulance was on its way, Mary said. She could hear the sirens in the air.

How was her daughter, the woman wanted to know. Was her daughter all right? She asked it over and over again.

Mary could not respond to the question. She could not bring herself to say what she knew.

Finally, a man from the crowd was able to release the seat belt and free the woman from her suspended position in the car. Gently she was lowered and extricated from the vehicle.

Mary stepped back when she felt that the woman was in good hands. She turned toward the corner and was startled not to see Elizabeth. For a moment her heart raced and she was short of breath, but, quickly scanning behind her, toward the body of the little girl, she saw Elizabeth, kneeling and praying.

Mary's eyes opened wide, however, at what else she saw. Her mouth fell open. There, beside Elizabeth, knelt a woman, bathed in bright light, dressed in pale blue ancient robes, with a simple white veil. Elizabeth's head was down, as if she were not aware of the presence of the woman.

Mary dropped to her knees at the sight. Truly, this woman was not of this earth.

In a moment, the woman was gone. Vanished.

THE MIRACLES

Elizabeth, though, remained in her praying position.

Mary rose and approached her daughter. As she got closer, she was astonished to notice a slight movement from the little girl's chest. She appeared to be breathing. Mary ran to her.

The child's eyes were closed. Mary touched her fingers gently to the girl's throat. Pulse. Ever so slight, but definite pulse.

CHAPTER ELEVEN

DAY THREE (Continued)

Mary tended to the pot roast and the vegetables on the stove as her mind drifted to the afternoon's events. The accident. The child. The lady bathed in light. It had been overwhelming.

Yet little Elizabeth had seemed so non-plused by it all. She had prayed to Our Blessed Lady, she had said.

The phone rang and it brought Mary back from her thoughts. She went to the side table near the couch to answer it.

"Hello," she said.

The male voice on the other end was soft-spoken: "Hello, is this Mrs. Depaul?"

"Yes."

THE MIRACLES

"Hi, Mrs. Depaul. My name is Randall Prens. I stopped by the other day and spoke with your husband."

"Yes. You're the reporter. He mentioned it."

"Did he tell you the nature of my interest?"

"Yes."

"That I was interested in knowing who visited you a couple of nights ago?"

"Yes."

"Well, I think it has been well established by my colleagues in the media at this point that the visitor was the Pope, though he, himself, has not confirmed that yet, nor, of course, have you or your husband. Nevertheless, with that background, you can imagine my reaction when I received a call a little while ago from a passerby to the auto accident this afternoon by the park near your house, and the passerby told me that there was a very strange happening at the scene."

Mary was silent.

"The passerby said that she overheard the name of the woman who helped. And it was you. And the passerby also said that your daughter was with you when you were talking with the police about the accident."

Still Mary was silent.

"Are you still there, Mrs. Depaul?"

"Yes."

"You were at the accident this afternoon, weren't you?"

"Yes."

"And your daughter was with you?"

"Yes."

"Let me ask you, Mrs. Depaul, did you notice anything strange while you were there? Anything at all? I mean, I know that it must have been quite a crash and I know that you helped the woman in the overturned vehicle -- you're a nurse, I understand, is that right?"

"Yes, I'm trained as a nurse."

"...but aside from the crash and the crowd and the ambulance and the police, did you notice anything strange today, Mrs. Depaul?"

"Strange?"

"Yes. Anything out of the ordinary."

"Like what?" She was stalling for time. Matthew had explained that he had been evasive with Prens in order to avoid any undue attention. A story in the press demanded attention and disrupted lives. Matthew had said that he wanted no part of it.

Prens was patient. If what he had learned was true, he could understand the reluctance to speak about it. He could not agree with it, but he could understand it.

"Like unusual lights, for example," he said. "Or unusual people."

Mary did not want to lie, yet she subscribed to Matthew's point that they would be better off without publicity. She knew only to be silent to avoid lying.

"Are you still there, Mrs. Depaul?"

"Yes."

"Let me ask you this, then: did your
daughter -- what's her name...Elizabeth, right?"

"Yes."

"...did Elizabeth kneel near the accident,
near the little girl who was thrown from the
car."

"Yes."

"And what was she doing?"

"She was praying for the little girl."

"I see." He was taking notes at a fast
clip. "And how old is Elizabeth?"

"She's six."

"I see. And when you noticed that she
was praying, did you think that unusual?"

"Unusual? Not at all. I prayed also."

"I see. Well, then, let me go back to my
original question: did you notice anything
unusual as Elizabeth was praying near the little
girl, anything at all?"

Mary was silent once more.

"Did you notice anything unusual at all
this afternoon?"

"Oh, my pot roast is burning, Mr. Prens.
I'm sorry, but I'll have to run."

"Please, Mrs. Depaul, before you go,
please hear me out. I understand your
reluctance to talk about it. I really do. But, as
I've indicated, others saw what you saw. And
they haven't been reluctant to talk. We have
much information and all I'm trying to do is get
some confirmation from you. But the story will
run tomorrow whether you make a statement or

not -- probably be front page. Your life is going
to change, whether you want it to or not. Your
whole family's life is going to change. I want to
give you an opportunity to set us all straight
about what is happening, so that rumors don't
get started, and so that others won't feel it
necessary to hound you for answers. And
believe me, they will. This is news, Mrs.
Depaul, and the people want to know. Please,
make a statement and help yourself. I promise
I'll be accurate and fair in reporting it."

Mary was silent.

"Even off the record, Mrs. Depaul. Tell
me what happened off the record and I will not
cite you in the story."

Silence.

"Please, Mrs. Depaul..."

She cut him off, careful to keep a polite
tone to her voice: "I'm sorry, Mr. Prens. I
really am. But I have to go now."

"Thank you for listening," he said.
"Please don't hesitate to call me if you change
your mind. I'm on your side."

That was not necessarily true. He
wanted the story. He wanted it very badly and
it didn't matter how he got it.

"I won't hesitate," she said. "Thank
you." She hung up.

She stood by the phone. "Your life is
going to change," he had said. "Your whole
family's life." Her hands began to grow a bit
sweaty. She did not want the attention that she
realized was inevitable. She had not been aware

that others saw the lady bathed in light. But they had. And now there would be a story. And now there would be attention. And now there would be change.

She closed her eyes to pray for guidance. She prayed that they would be able to manage.

CHAPTER TWELVE

DAY THREE (Continued)

Mary dished the potatoes on to Matthew's plate. The dinner table had been uncommonly quiet for the past few minutes: all three in this family seemed just a bit preoccupied in thought tonight.

With the dinner before them, they made the sign of the cross, linked themselves by holding hands, and Matthew prayed aloud. "Thank you, God, for this wonderful meal and this wonderful family. Let us always remember those who are less fortunate than we are. Let us always try to be holy, healthy and happy."

He paused and looked to Elizabeth. "Would you like to add anything?" he asked.

THE MIRACLES

She looked up with her big brown eyes. At first it appeared that she would decline, but eventually she accepted. "May the Blessed Virgin watch over us and may the little girl and her mother in the accident this afternoon get better real soon."

"Amen," said Mary.

They began to eat.

"They will be getting better soon," said Mary. "I called my friend, Dottie, at the hospital and she said it was miraculous -- given the impact and all -- but that she thought they might be released in just a day or so."

"It was miraculous, now wasn't it," said Matthew. He glanced at Elizabeth from the side of his eye.

She caught it and knew that he was addressing himself to her.

"Our Lady answers prayers, Daddy," Elizabeth said. "I prayed today and she answered me."

"And so I heard," said Matthew. "I heard that she not only answered you, but that she also visited with you."

"Strange," said Elizabeth, "but I was so busy praying that I never saw her at all."

"She had her eyes closed the whole time," said Mary.

"But I could feel her presence," said Elizabeth. "She *is* such a wonderful lady."

Matthew shook his head. "We have so much to be thankful for."

The Christmas tree, now all decorated with lights and ornaments and garland, caught Mary's eye. "The tree looks so good," she said.

Matthew and Elizabeth turned their attention to it.

"We did a great job," said Matthew.

Elizabeth focused on the very top, the bare branch which stuck up toward the ceiling. "It'll look better when we put something on the top."

"How about a red bow?" said Mary.

"Or a star?" said Matthew. "I can try to pick up a star on 5th Avenue."

"Would it be possible to get an angel?" Elizabeth asked. "I really think it would look best with an angel."

Matthew shrugged his shoulders. "I'll see what they have at the store."

Elizabeth's expression seemed to show a bit of disappointment that he did not share her enthusiasm for an angel. Mary noticed.

The phone rang and Mary made an immediate move for it. "Now doesn't this person calling know that we're eating."

Elizabeth smiled.

"I'll be back before my potatoes stop steaming," Mary said.

She picked up the receiver on the table near the couch. "Hello."

She listened for a moment, ready to tell the caller at the first available chance that dinner was on the table, but as she listened her jaw dropped a bit and her eyes opened wide. "I can't believe it," she said.

At that, both Matthew and Elizabeth turned toward her.

"That's...that's..." She couldn't find the right word. "...that's great, that's wonderful, that's just the best news I could imagine hearing."

She listened for another moment, smiling now, beaming, in fact.

"I'll call you later," she said.

In a daze of thoughts, she padded slowly back to the table to rejoin the family.

Matthew assumed it was Dottie with more news from the hospital about the mother and daughter in the accident. "Was that Dottie?" he asked.

Mary did not hear him, still lost in the conversation, still staring blankly.

"Was that Dottie?" he asked again, a little louder this time.

She heard him. "No," she said softly. "No, that was Barbara." She looked to Elizabeth. "Your Aunt Barbara's baby is alive. She went to the doctor and he said it was impossible to explain, but the baby is not dead after all. It's definitely alive and very vibrant and everything seems to be as it should be."

Matthew's mouth dropped a bit.

Elizabeth was smiling.

CHAPTER THIRTEEN

DAY THREE (CONTINUED)

The man dressed all in black, surrounded by an entourage also in black, walked at a slow but deliberate pace through the airport terminal. Clearly, the man in the center, like the Queen Bee of a hive, was the focus of attention and care, the others hustling around him as they walked, talking to him, tending to him.

The man in the center, his thinning white hair parted neatly to the side, his broad shoulders somewhat bent, seeming to be carrying the weight of many on them, made a point of tending to each of his entourage as well as each was tending to him. When he was spoken to, he turned his kind, blue eyes to the person speaking, devoting his undivided attention to him. His eyes hinted at a quiet and gentle nature, the nature to be expected of the Vicar of Christ on earth.

The entourage did not notice the man in gray as they passed him. He stood to the side, leaning against the wall, a newspaper up to shield his face. But as the entourage passed, he lowered the paper just enough to glare at the man in the center. This was no glare of curiosity, but rather a venomous glare, from deep black eyes under bushy, slanted brows.

The entourage moved at its deliberate pace out of the terminal and into a waiting limousine. The man in gray followed as closely as he could without being noticed and when they had left, he moved straight to the nearest pay phone and made a call.

CHAPTER FOURTEEN

DAY FOUR

The sun had not risen yet. It would not rise for another two hours or so. But Mary was awake, lying quietly in bed, thinking, watching in the dark. So much was happening so quickly in her life, in her family's lives. Her sleep patterns had been disrupted and, while she was normally an early riser anyhow, she was waking much earlier these days.

The ringing phone near her side of the bed startled her. Who on earth, she thought, could be calling at this hour of the morning?

"Hello."

"Hello, is this Mrs. Depaul?"

"Yes."

THE MIRACLES

"My name is Jerry Dunbar. I'm a producer with Channel Two News and I was wondering if I could make an appointment with you to have a crew come to your house this morning to interview you and your daughter."

"Interview me and my daughter? Why?" She knew the answer before he had a chance to give it.

"Well, about the apparition..."

She noted that it was the first time the word had been used. Even Randall Prens, the newspaper reporter, had not used it when she spoke to him.

"...at the accident."

"I'm not sure I know what you're talking about."

"Oh...well, the story's on the front page of the newspaper...I thought..."

"Mr. Dunbar, I'm sorry to seem uncooperative, but we won't be giving any interviews. Thank you for your interest, really, but we don't have anything to say."

"I understand," he said. "I'm terribly sorry for having disturbed you so early."

He sounded sincere. She had not felt the same sincerity in Randall Prens' voice.

"Thank you," she said. "If anything changes, I'll call you."

"You have the name, right? Jerry Dunbar..."

"I have your name, she said, "Channel Two News."

"Right. Would you like the telephone number?"

"That won't be necessary"

"Oh, okay."

They each said goodbye and she hung up.

She looked over at Matthew, still sound asleep. She wasn't surprised that he had not woken up. He could sleep through a hurricane.

She got up from the bed, took the white flannel robe from the chair nearby, and covered herself as she padded out of the room and into the hall. She peeked into Elizabeth's room. Sound asleep, with her covers sprawled away from her, hanging to the floor. Mary could not help smiling at her. Fluffy lay at the foot of the bed.

Down the stairs Mary went, straight to the front door. She fumbled with the chain-lock and was disappointed that she was making more noise than she wanted to make. She did not want to wake the others. Finally able to get the door unlocked and open, she peered out into the dark, canvassing the stoop with her squinted eyes, searching for the newspaper. She spotted it.

She hustled into the December morning chill in her white flannel robe, swooped up the paper and hustled back inside so quickly and deftly as to remind anyone who saw her of a football player scooping up a fumbled football and scurrying into the end zone.

THE MIRACLES

Back inside, she re-locked the door and glanced down at the paper as she made her way to the kitchen table. It did not take long to find the article. There, sprawled across the front page, read the headline: "DOZENS REPORT APPARITION AT ACCIDENT SITE." As expected, the article was written by Randall Prens.

Mechanically, she found her chair at the table and sat as she devoured the story beneath the headline. Nearly everyone present at the accident, it seemed, had seen the woman bathed in light, dressed in blue robes and a white veil, kneeling by the little girl. Elizabeth was identified in the first paragraph. Prens made it clear that the "vision" and Elizabeth were praying side by side.

Prens focused the middle paragraphs on the woman. "Beautiful," "dazzling," "from the heavens," came the descriptions from those present. One woman witness left no doubt at all as to who she thought it was: "Mary, Our Blessed Lady," she said.

Prens played it up, describing the ethereal nature of the scene, citing other apparitions in New York, in other states and in other countries recently. Yet Mary could not shake the sense that Prens did not believe what he was reporting. There was something about the tone that sounded doubtful and distrusting.

Nearing the end of the story, Prens re-focused on Elizabeth. Was "Mary, the Blessed Lady" going to appear again to pray by

Elizabeth's side? Did Elizabeth have some special connection to the heavens? Was this a sign and could Elizabeth shed light on its significance?

Mary shook her head upon completing the article. It was no wonder that the TV producer had called. Prens had written the story in such a way as to make Elizabeth a much sought-after interview.

Mary's mind raced and she tried to clear it enough to foresee the day ahead. There would be other TV producers, other reporters, calling, coming around. "Your life is going to change," Prens had said, and she knew he was right -- at least temporarily.

She sat there at the kitchen table, staring into space and running her hands slowly through her hair. Dawn broke out through the window behind her. She sat wistfully, trying to clear her head, trying to prepare for the day. Closing her eyes, she prayed for guidance and strength.

CHAPTER FIFTEEN

DAY FOUR (Continued)

Matthew peeked through the curtains of his bedroom window. The skies were clear, the light of the morning strong.

But the clear skies were not the reason Matthew was peeking through the window. In the street below was an assembly of reporters, photographers, tech crews and police. He could see Randall Prens, scooping his blonde hair from his eyes, standing in the middle of the street, talking to a photographer. Two TV station vans, with satellite dishes atop, sat parked one-behind-the-other on the far side of the street.

Matthew reviewed the conversation he had had earlier that morning with the police sergeant on duty. It would be best, the sergeant had said, if someone from the family could make a statement. He knew this from experience, he had said. While a statement would not necessarily get rid of the entire lot, most of them would be satisfied. A few would linger, however, hoping for a photo of the girl, or -- bigger yet -- for another apparition!

Matthew had agreed. He would make a statement -- a very brief statement -- at 10:00 A.M..

He looked at his watch: 9:55.

He went downstairs. Mary and Elizabeth were tinkering with the Christmas tree, adjusting ornaments.

"Are you ready for this?" Mary asked.

"As I'll ever be," he said.

He looked at Elizabeth's big brown eyes. They seemed sympathetic.

"I love you, Daddy," she said. She was hugging her little Fluffy.

He smiled. "I love you, too, sweetie." She did seem especially sweet to him this morning. He loved it when her hair was in pigtails.

She was wearing a pink top and pink pants and she was holding Fluffy so dearly. "I hope they're nice to you out there," she said. "They seemed all pushy and shovey this morning when Mom opened the door for a minute."

"I'm sure they'll be nice."

THE MIRACLES

He walked to the door, took a deep breath, and went out. The December air was crisp, but the morning sun made it quite tolerable. And there was plenty of sun.

At the sight of Matthew, the dozens of reporters and photographers and technical support people rushed to the police officer stationed at the bottom of the stoop. He stood now between the media and Matthew.

Cameras flashed as reporters shouted questions for Matthew. The cacophony was so pronounced that he could not make out a one of them. He could see Randall Prens near the front of the pack. His lips were moving, but Matthew could not discern what he was saying.

Matthew raised his hands and asked them to let him speak, and, as if their lives depended on it, they quieted quickly in compliance. Matthew was a bit surprised at the power of his word. He amused himself with the wish that they would comply if he simply asked them to leave.

Dozens of microphones, many of them emblazoned with the call letters of TV and radio stations, were set up on a makeshift stand at the base of the stairs, and Matthew approached them. He was glad that he could look out to the crowd and speak to all present. He cleared his throat. "I have no practice speaking to groups," he said. "I hope you will be patient. I'll try to give you a statement that you can use, but I can't promise that I'll be giving you necessarily what you want."

Though a few in the crowd frowned at that, still all were quiet.

Matthew continued: "My daughter, Elizabeth, and my wife, Mary, were at the scene of the auto accident near the park yesterday. Both were very moved by the distress of the victims. My wife tried to help the woman in the car. My daughter went to the side of the little girl lying in the street. We believe in prayer. Both my daughter and my wife prayed that the woman and the child would be all right."

He hesitated and scanned the crowd before him. Seeing the hungry looks in their eyes, he wished he had prepared more. "That's about it."

Simultaneously, as if one, they moved closer to him and the police officer, hard pressed to keep a space between them and Matthew, signaled to a colleague to join him, and he did. The two uniformed men stood fast.

"What did they see?" came a shout.

"Was there an apparition of some kind?" came another.

"How old is your daughter?" a woman in the front asked.

Matthew focused on her. "She's six," he said.

The woman was quick to take advantage of his attention, and most of the other reporters gave her the floor, some sticking their hand-held microphones close to her mouth, some scribbling furiously on their pads. "We have reports," said the woman, "that at one point in the minutes following the accident, there was an unexplained bright light. Can you tell us if your daughter or your wife saw the light?"

"My wife did say she saw a light, yes. My daughter had her eyes closed and didn't see anything."

"There were reports also of a woman in the light. Did your wife see the woman?"

"I believe she did."

"When will we get a chance to speak with your wife and daughter?"

Matthew smiled. "You can see how difficult this is for me. I know you all mean well, but I'm sure you can understand how apprehensive someone might be at the prospect of speaking to a group like this. I'm sure you can appreciate our wanting to keep a low profile. We're not seeking any attention..."

He could see that the woman was not satisfied and he realized that he had not answered the question specifically enough.

"...and, so, I've been designated the spokesperson for the family, and neither my wife nor my daughter will be making any statements."

Suddenly, a flurry of flashes from every camera in the crowd startled Matthew and caused him to squint. The reporters squeezed closer and the police officers strained to keep them back. A third police officer joined them to assist.

Matthew was confused. He could not understand the reporters' reaction. He was utterly baffled -- until he realized that their focus was behind him.

He turned to see Elizabeth in the doorway. She seemed so innocent, so vulnerable, all dressed in pink, with pigtails, her bangs cut neatly across her forehead, her big brown eyes so wide.

Matthew made a move toward her, but stopped when he saw that she seemed not at all aware of him nor of the crowd of reporters, but, rather, that she was staring into the sky, oddly, with tilted head, her eyes searching, searching. The reporters also noticed her behavior and, rather than fire a barrage of questions at her, they stayed back and watched her every move, waiting to see what she would do.

Matthew could see that Mary was behind her, just inside the doorway, and he felt a bit better for it, knowing that Mary was aware of what was happening. But what, indeed, was happening, Matthew wondered. Why was Elizabeth out here?

Without warning a bright light descended from the sky and the crowd gasped in amazement and fear. Elizabeth knelt and the light fixed itself in the air just above the doorway. The little child put her hands together in prayer and stared directly at the light, which the others could not do for its intensity.

A few of the reporters fell to their knees, but most remained as poised as possible, some scribbling in their notepads, some speaking softly into their microphones. No fewer than four video cameramen were capturing the entire scene on tape. Two photographers were frozen in awe, their cameras dormant, hanging toward the ground in their outstretched hands.

Matthew held his place and knelt on the stairs, facing Elizabeth and the light. Its intensity was blinding and he could do no more than squint. He could hardly see Elizabeth, but he could see Mary inside the doorway: she, too, was on her knees, squinting.

The crowd reacted with hushed "oooohs" when the bright white light suspended above the door suddenly took on a glow around its perimeter, with golden rays shining from it in all directions. The rays shimmered and moved slowly around the outside of the body of light.

Elizabeth's mouth was moving, as if in prayer, but Matthew could hear no words. She stared straight into the light above her and when she was not praying she seemed to be listening. She smiled.

Without warning, it began to rain. Matthew and the others looked to the sky and were amazed to see that there was not a cloud in sight. Yet it was raining! Matthew was not alone in wondering how it could rain without clouds. It was a light rain at first, then grew heavier and heavier.

No one in the crowd was dressed for rain. No umbrellas were visible. With each

increase in the intensity of the rain, one or two
from the crowd ran for cover in their cars or
vans, but most stayed exactly where they were,
fixed on the light, still speaking softly
occasionally into their microphones or
scribbling away on their wet pads. Some did
nothing but stare, motionless, silent. All were
getting soaked.

Elizabeth was entirely focused on the
light and appeared to be having an enjoyable
conversation. She went from talking to
listening, to talking to listening, all the time
smiling.

And then, as quickly as the rain had
come, it was gone. In less time than it takes to
snap fingers, the rain stopped abruptly. The sky
had not changed at all, still clear and cloudless,
with no hint of foul weather.

A quick moment after the rain had
stopped, the light began to ascend toward the
sky. The golden rays shone brightly from its
perimeter for a while and then disappeared. In
a second the light, itself, was gone.

The crowd of reporters were stunned
and did not move for a moment, transfixed on
the light, trying to absorb what was happening.
But it did not take long until one stirred, then
another, then another, and ultimately a hum of
chatter came from them, as each conferred with
others to verify what had transpired.

Elizabeth stayed kneeling in the
doorway. She had watched the light ascend to

the heavens and when it disappeared, she closed her eyes in thoughtful prayer.

Randall Prens moved toward her and one of the police officers stepped in his path. Another reporter moved forward also, then another and another, until the throng in its entirety was again straining toward the little girl, shouting questions to her, flashing cameras at her, taking video of her.

Elizabeth stayed fast in her spot in the doorway, on her knees in prayer. When she opened her eyes after a moment she seemed surprised that there was even a crowd, let alone that it was shouting at her and taking her picture.

She began to rise slowly and Mary moved in behind her to lead her inside. But Elizabeth turned to Mary and said a few words, and the both of them stayed in place for a moment. Mary turned to Matthew with an expression that made him know she wanted him. He rose and went up the stairs to the doorway.

"She wants to speak to them," Mary said.

Matthew looked at Elizabeth. She was so little, so innocent. Could she speak to this hungry crowd of veteran, cynical reporters? "Why do you want to speak to them?" Matthew asked.

"Because she asked me to talk to them."
"Who asked you?"
"The Blessed Virgin."

93

"Did you see her?"

"Yes, Daddy. You couldn't see her, could you?"

"No. I could only see a light, a very bright light."

"She said that. She said that everyone would know that she was here, but that I was the only one who could actually see her."

"What else did the Blessed Virgin say?" Mary asked.

"Well, she said that I should give a message to everyone who is here."

Matthew looked at Mary. "I guess it'll be all right," he said.

Mary nodded.

Matthew led Elizabeth down the stairs to the bank of microphones, and when the crowd saw that she was coming down they quieted slightly. One video cameraman, seeing that the little girl would not be able to reach the cluster of microphones, offered the portable footstool that he had been using to shoot over the heads in the crowd. Matthew accepted it and set it before the stand. Elizabeth stepped up.

She did not seem a bit nervous. She had barely turned six years of age and she was facing a crowd of reporters who were filled with questions and mixed feelings about what they, themselves, had just witnessed, but she was poised, relaxed, not the least bit burdened with anxiety.

THE MIRACLES

The cameras flashed, the reporters scribbled, and the video tapes rolled. All were impressed with this poise.

Even on the stand, Elizabeth had to strain just a bit to reach up to the microphones. "I just spoke with the Blessed Virgin Mary," she said, and the flashing and scribbling and rolling intensified. "That was her in the light."

Every bit of energy in the crowd was focused on the little girl straining at the microphones.

Elizabeth continued: "She said that you would know that she was here, but that you would not be able to see her."

Matthew looked at his daughter as she spoke and tears came to his eyes. She was so small, so cute with her pigtails and her bangs and her pink outfit. And she was so blessed.

"She asked me to give you a message," Elizabeth said.

The silence of the crowd was deafening. All eyes and cameras were fixed on this little child. Many were holding their breath and did not even realize it.

"She wants you to pray. She wants the world to pray. Pray that people return to God. She wants you to pray to her son, Jesus. Ask him to help. People have turned away from God, she said, and it makes her and her son very sad. She wants us all to pray that people will love God and do what God wants us to do."

Elizabeth was silent for a moment and it appeared that she was finished.

The same woman who had spoken up before and who had been able to get Matthew's attention, spoke up now. "And what does God want us to do?" she asked.

"The Blessed Virgin said that you would know the answer to that in your hearts. She said that God's message has been here with us on earth for a long time. It's a simple message of love. Love Him and love each other."

The crowd marveled at this little girl, speaking well beyond her years. It was difficult to imagine that she was only six. But most understood that these were not her words, that she was merely relaying this message.

Randall Prens spoke up: "You said that they are sad. Why are they sad?"

Elizabeth did not need to hesitate for a response. "Because people have not shown their love. The earth is filled with....I'm not exactly sure what this means, but the Blessed Virgin said that you would know...the earth is filled with moral decay. People need to turn to God, turn to Jesus and ask for help."

There was silence for a moment, until it was clear that Elizabeth was not going to continue with the thought. And then Prens spoke up again. "Did she say anything else?"

Elizabeth shook her head. "No. Except..."

All the pens and cameras stayed poised.

"...except that she would be back." The pens scribbled furiously and the cameras flashed and whirred.

"When?" a voice asked from the rear of the crowd.

"Tomorrow morning. She didn't say exactly when."

"What did she look like?" someone wanted to know.

Elizabeth smiled. "She's beautiful. She's more beautiful than any of the paintings of her. She's in a bright light with stars around her head."

"Why is she appearing to you?" Prens asked.

"She didn't tell me that."

"Why isn't she appearing to us?" a woman asked.

Elizabeth shook her head and hunched her shoulders to say that she did not know.

Matthew sensed that it was time to go inside. Elizabeth was smiling, but she did seem a bit drained from the experience. He knew the crowd would ask questions forever if they had a chance.

He hoisted her into his arms and leaned in toward the microphones. "Thank you. I'm sure you would agree that you received more today than you ever imagined you would. We won't have anything more to say now."

The flurry of questions continued, overlapping now, no one caring to be polite at this point, but Matthew tuned them out. His only goal at this point was to bring his daughter safely inside. The crowd pressed forward but the police officers were effective in holding their ground.

Matthew took Elizabeth up the stairs and into the doorway, where Mary stood waiting. She closed the door behind them. Matthew put his arm around Mary and the three of them hugged silently for several moments. Nothing needed to be said. This was, indeed, a special day, and this family had been blessed.

CHAPTER SIXTEEN

DAY FOUR (Continued)

The woman reporter on the television screen was looking directly into the camera. In the background was the front of the Depaul house on 77th Street. Over the reporter's shoulder now a small box appeared and in the box was a rolling videotape of Elizabeth standing in the doorway, at first looking upward and then kneeling and praying.

"...and Elizabeth Depaul, who just turned six years of age, knelt in her doorway and, as I said before, a light appeared in the sky and descended to the top of the doorway -- I assure you that all who were present, and that included at least 20 reporters and crew from television, radio, and newspapers from the metropolitan area, saw this light, although, very oddly, it does not appear in this taped footage. No one can explain why. Cameramen from three other television crews also recorded the scene, but the light did not appear on their tape either. And photographs that were taken by media and others at the scene did not capture the light."

Matthew, Mary, and Elizabeth sat on their couch, watching the news report on the television. They were awed by seeing their own images for the first time on the screen and they were as surprised as the reporter about the videotape, showing the scene without the light.

Matthew offered his thoughts: "For many people it's not necessary to actually see the light in order to know that something very special, something miraculous, happened here today."

Mary spoke up: "It's a good example of the importance of having faith -- how you can't always prove something, even though you know it's true. Everyone present saw the light. They know it was there, but they can't prove it."

"Our Lady said that the blessed would know she was present," said Elizabeth.

The reporter continued: "The light was very bright and it took on a golden edge with golden rays. Many who were present, including media, dropped to their knees in awe and, yes, some even in worship."

THE MIRACLES

The rolling videotape in the box over her shoulder, showed the scene as she described it.

"Elizabeth, the little girl, knelt in her doorway, looking up at the light, which was too bright for anyone else present to look at directly, and she prayed. Later, when the light disappeared, rising up toward the sky, little Elizabeth told of what she saw..."

In the box now was a tape of Elizabeth at the microphones. Matthew, Mary, and Elizabeth continued to watch the television in silence, their mouths open slightly, their eyes wide.

Near the end of Elizabeth's report to the reporters, when she said that the Blessed Virgin would be back the next morning, Matthew spoke up again: "Knowing that there's going to be another apparition, those reporters will stick around now."

"And there'll be more of them," said Mary.

When the news report was over, Matthew got up from the couch and went to the window to peek out into the street. His eyes widened at what he saw. There, across the street, right behind the fire hydrant, near Mrs. Mulrooney's house, was a scaffold with a platform, and on the platform were two cameramen and their equipment. The television networks were now on the scene.

Matthew shook his head. This would be more significant than he had imagined. Much more significant.

CHAPTER SEVENTEEN

DAY FOUR (Continued)

Mary was on the phone when Matthew entered the living room.

"...and thanks again, Mrs. Vicenzo," said Mary. "We really appreciate your help." She hung up.

Matthew sat on the couch and Mary plopped herself down beside him. They needed a moment of rest in this hectic day. He put his arm around her lovingly, as they appreciated the decorations on the Christmas tree.

"Mrs. Vicenzo said it's fine with her," Mary said.

"Great."

"And she'll leave the gate on the other side unlocked."

Matthew smiled. "I never thought in a million years that I would ever have to sneak out of my own house, and through my neighbor's yard."

Mary shook her head. "It's either that or stay home from now on."

"Or fight through the mob in front," he added.

She nodded in agreement

Elizabeth, still with her pigtails and her pink outfit from earlier, bounced down the stairs and joined them on the couch. "Are we going soon?" she asked.

"How about right now," Matthew said as he sprang to his feet. "This seems as good a time as any to make a run for it."

He was smirking and Mary caught the sarcasm. "If it weren't so sad," she said, "it'd be pretty darned funny."

Matthew made a face that acknowledged that she was right. "It is sad," he said sheepishly.

The late afternoon sun was peeking through the drawn curtains. Matthew retrieved three jackets from the closet by the door and walked with deliberate steps away from the window, not wanting to risk any of the reporters from outside even catching a glimpse of what he was doing.

They donned their jackets and made their way to the back door. Matthew led the way. He peered out into the yard and motioned to the others that all was clear.

THE MIRACLES

They left the house and walked quickly to the three-foot, wire fence separating their property from Mrs. Vicenzo's. Matthew hopped over it and leaned back over to lift Elizabeth to him. That done, he helped Mary over, too.

They walked through Mrs. Vicenzo's yard toward the gate on the opposite side.

"Don't step on the flower bed," Mary said. "Mrs. Vicenzo asked us to be very careful about that."

Matthew led them away from the flower bed, which, at this time of the year had no flowers anyway. Just the same, he thought, it was better to avoid the bed all together.

Mrs. Vicenzo was in her window and waved to them as they passed her. Her well-decorated Christmas tree was visible behind her. Elizabeth waved back, as Matthew and Mary smiled acknowledgement. The gate was unlocked, as Mrs. Vicenzo had said it would be, and the look on her face seemed to say: "See, I lived up to my word."

A cement path led them behind the next house and beyond it to an alley that ran parallel to the street. They walked the length of the alley, behind a row of tenements, and in a moment they had reached another alley on the right, running perpendicular to the first. Matthew led them through it and on to 77th Street, well away from their house, almost to 5th Avenue.

Mary put on sunglasses in a minor effort
to disguise herself. She knew it was not much,
but she felt that she had to do something. She
picked up Elizabeth to keep attention away
from her: she knew that any journalist on the
block -- and, for that matter, even within five
miles -- would be alert to the presence of a little
girl about six years of age. She carried her for a
while and put her down when they reached the
avenue.

They walked at a fairly quick pace the
few blocks to the church, through the streets of
Bay Ridge, past tenement after tenement,
alternating with rows and rows of brownstones
with their long stoops swooping down from the
second floor to the street level. Holiday
decorations were everywhere -- colored bulbs
hung from streetlights, blinking lights framed
windows and doors, and Christmas trees were
visible in living rooms along the way. Along
4th Avenue it was one architecturally grand
apartment house after another, each with its
own distinct characteristics -- four stories high,
six stories high, red brick, white brick, columns
here, corner-supports there, large courtyard in
front, small courtyard in front.

When they arrived at the church they
were pleased to see Father Dunne in front,
speaking with an elderly woman with
weathered, olive skin. She wore a simple black
dress and a gray kerchief over her head.

Father Dunne, his gray hair a bit swept
by a soft wind, and his glasses poised at the tip

of his nose, saw them approaching and seemed genuinely thrilled. He cut short his conversation with the elderly woman and greeted the trio as they climbed the steps of the church.

"I'm so glad to see you," Father Dunne said. "I've been trying to reach you all day but your phone just keeps ringing and ringing."

Mary was apologetic: "We've had to ignore the phone, Father. I hope you understand. It hasn't stopped ringing since..."

The priest was nodding and did not need to hear any more. "Of course, of course. I figured as much."

"We've had calls from the media, from friends, from businesses -- one corporation even wanted to talk to us about a licensing agreement for T-shirts."

Father Dunne continued to nod sympathetically. "Where there's a buck," he said.

Mary frowned and shook her head in disgust.

"I was going to take a walk over to see you later today anyhow," said the priest, "and so I'm glad to see you now. You must have had to fight your way through the crowd of journalists outside your door."

Matthew was shaking his head. "We avoided them for now, but something tells me it's going to become increasingly difficult to avoid them in the future."

Father Dunne nodded in understanding and in sympathy. "Come inside," he said, motioning them to follow.

The elderly woman stalled nearby, eyeing the visitors with curiosity. She watched them as they made their way into the church.

Queen of All Saints Church -- its parishioners called it by its letters: "Q-A-S" -- was uncharacteristically void of visitors at this hour. A huge church, with floor-to-ceiling, marble columns on each side, QAS was a very popular locus. The tiles on the floor glistened in the soft light and the ceilings were extraordinarily high.. With enormous stained glass windows and well-polished pews from front to back, the church in "normal" times was hardly ever empty. It was not at all uncommon to see dozens of visitors at off hours during the day.

Mary noticed. "I'm surprised no one's here," she said.

Father Dunne grimaced. "The police advised us of another burglary in the neighborhood," he said. "We've had to cut back on the hours. It's a shame, but we just can't risk leaving it open and unattended. It's too vulnerable. We'll be putting the revised hours in this week's bulletin."

Mary glanced at the three altars at the front of the church -- one grand altar with golden tabernacle in the center, and two well-appointed but smaller altars to each side. All were adorned with much gold and other

precious metals. She could understand well the
church's need to take precautions.

Mary, Matthew, and Elizabeth stayed
with Father Dunne at the rear of the church.
They had come in search of spiritual guidance.

"We would be grateful for any advice,"
said Mary.

The gray-haired priest put his hand atop
little Elizabeth's head. "You have been blessed
like no others," he said. "The only advice I can
offer is to follow your hearts." He knelt to
speak directly to Elizabeth. "You are a very
special little girl."

She was silent but her eyes said that she
understood that she had been given something
special. She knew.

"Our Lady loves you very much." Father
Dunne continued, "to show herself to you like
this. I saw on the television how you spoke to
the crowd in front of your house and you did
such a wonderful job. I can't think of anything
specific to tell you, but I do want you to know
that I'll be available to you at any time, night or
day, in case you want to speak with me or ask
me something."

She nodded. "Thank you, Father."

He stood up and addressed himself to
Mary and Matthew. "It is I and others who will
be seeking advice from you and Elizabeth."

His visitors knew he was right. Though
reluctant, they were now cast in new and
unfamiliar roles. "We're concerned about the
crowds and the attention," Matthew said.

"And it promises to grow," said the priest.

Matthew nodded. "I've been careful to protect the family as best I could so far, Father, but I wonder if we should be taking advantage of this attention to get the word out. This is a great opportunity to speak into the cameras and spread God's word."

"It could not have been spread any better than Elizabeth spread it this morning. Our Lady will guide you. When she returns, she will have another message. Elizabeth will know what to do, just as she knew today."

Mary spoke up. "It's going to be difficult to keep it from becoming a circus. Already the networks have set up platforms and scaffolds for their cameras across from our house."

Father Dunne put his arm on her shoulder. "Our Lady is doing this for a reason. Indeed, she does want the word to receive attention. I dare say that by the time you return, there may be more platforms to accommodate not just the American networks, but the world's networks. The Blessed Virgin appearing to a little child is news that cannot be held down. Let them come. Let them set up their platforms. Our Lady will guide you."

"But our lives," Matthew said. "Our everyday lives are going to have to be halted. I've had to take an emergency leave from my job because I can't feel comfortable going off to work and leaving Mary and Elizabeth alone to handle the mob. You know our financial situation, Father. We can't afford any loss of income. And we've even had to sneak out of our own house to come to see you."

Mary's face reflected her concern. "We're thinking of not sending Elizabeth to school for a while...at least until this all settles down somehow."

"That's probably a good idea," said the priest. "She'll be getting an education unlike any available to her in school." He patted Elizabeth's head. "She's an intelligent young lady. She'll be fine. A little bit of home-schooling from Mom and Dad will be as good, if not better than her regular routine." He looked at the little girl. "Right?"

She smiled. "Right, Father."

Mary's face still showed a bit of concern and the priest was sensitive to it.

"And I'll tell you what," he said. "After a little while, if things don't settle down enough to make you comfortable, I'll make arrangements with some friends of mine upstate who can put you up and give you a little anonymity. It'll be like a vacation."

That made Mary's eyes show a bit of relief. "That sounds great, Father. Thank you."

He smiled. "Trust in God. This is a special time for you and it would be so much better, if it were at all possible, to put your worries on the side and focus on the joy of the moment."

Mary smiled back.

"You're welcome to stay, if you'd like," said the priest. "I have an appointment with the Bishop in a little while, but I'm free for the rest of the evening after that."

"Thanks, Father," said Matthew, "but I think it would be best if we went back now, while we still have the afternoon light."

"Of course," Father Dunne said as he turned toward the doors. "But the offer holds. If you change your minds -- tonight or any time -- just let me know."

"We will," said Matthew. "Thanks again."

They walked slowly to the doors. "Speaking of the Bishop," said Father Dunne, "I'm sure he'll want to speak with you all at some point, but I don't expect it's urgent at the moment. I'll speak with him in a little while and find out what he's thinking."

"That would be great, Father," said Mary.

They went out of the church and stalled by the doors to say their goodbyes. The elderly woman with the black dress and the gray kerchief was still standing nearby, and when she saw them emerge, she approached.

"I know you," she said, looking at Elizabeth. "You're the little girl who spoke with the Blessed Virgin."

Father Dunne stepped forward to cut her off, but the elderly woman would not be denied. She rushed past the priest as if he were not even there, and when she reached Elizabeth

she knelt. "Please pray for my Agnes," she said.
"Please...please pray to the Blessed Mother for
my Agnes." She laid her hand gently on
Elizabeth's arm.

Father Dunne stood by the woman's side
and explained: "This is Mrs. Yuroslavak.
Agnes is her daughter. She's in the hospital
with a brain tumor and the doctors don't think
she has much longer to live."

"Please," said the woman again, "please
pray to the Blessed Mother for my Agnes."

Though Mary and Matthew hesitated,
not knowing exactly how to respond, Elizabeth
did not hesitate to comply, kneeling next to the
woman to pray, closing her eyes in silent
concentration. They stayed like that for a few
minutes, the two of them, kneeling together,
and tears rolled down the wrinkled, weathered,
olive cheeks of Mrs. Yuroslavak.

When Elizabeth was finished praying,
she opened her eyes and stood. She smiled at
the elderly woman by her side, who thanked her
profusely in between short bursts of emotion
and crying.

As Father Dunne tended to Mrs.
Yuroslavak, Mary and Matthew led Elizabeth
down the steps of the church.

"I'll be in touch," said Father Dunne.

Mary and Matthew nodded and
Elizabeth waved as they started on their trip
back to their home. The sun had just set and
the sky was breathless shades of red before
them as they walked. They travelled at a

113

measured pace, not wanting to go too fast to attract attention, yet anxious to get home. Mary donned her sunglasses.

Again they passed the grand apartment houses along 4th Avenue and the long stoops of the brownstones on the side streets. Again they marveled at the holiday decorations adorning the streets and the homes.

They were nearing the tenements bordering 5th Avenue when, at the very last brownstone of the row, they noticed a man with dark glasses and a German shepherd coming slowly down the long set of stairs leading from the house's second floor. The dog was harnessed and the man was grasping the railing quite firmly, a clear indication that he was blind.

Just as Mary, Matthew and Elizabeth reached the brownstone, the man lost his footing on the stairway and tumbled hard the three or four steps to the bottom. The shepherd jumped to the side, out of the way.

Matthew ran to the aid of the fallen blind man, and knelt beside him to assess the injuries, if any. "Are you all right?" Matthew asked.

"Yes," came the reply. "I think so." The man -- Matthew guessed him to be in his mid 40's -- propped himself slowly on one elbow to take stock. "Thank you for your help; I'm so embarrassed."

By this time Mary and Elizabeth had joined Matthew at the man's side.

THE MIRACLES

"Please don't be embarrassed," Matthew said. "This happens to all of us every now and then. In fact, I fell down my stairs just a few days ago."

The man was not certain whether it was true, but he was grateful for the gesture from this Good Samaritan. "I guess so," he said simply, and he left it at that. He took a deep breath and seemed to be calmed by the presence of someone to help. "Henry?" he called, and it was clear immediately that he was calling to his dog. Mary realized it and assured him that the shepherd was standing faithfully nearby.

Comforted, and recovered enough to try to regain his feet, the man pushed up from his elbow and sat up straight. Then, slowly, he climbed up from the ground. Matthew and Mary, one on each side of the man, supported him under his arms as he rose.

Elizabeth, also wanting to help, clasped his wrist to offer what stability she could. He realized that he was being helped by a child and he offered a special thanks to her as he stood.

Once straightened, he bent forward toward the child. "And what's your name?" he asked gently.

"Elizabeth."

"Well, Elizabeth, I want you to know that you have helped to make my day."

"Thank you."

"No, it's I who should thank you, Elizabeth. And the best way that I can think of to thank you is to give you a little gift."

Mary spoke up: "Oh, that won't be necessary, really..."

"Please," said the man, "it will make me feel much better. It's not a gift that you can touch, though. It's much more valuable than that."

Elizabeth's eyes said that she was curious now.

"I'm going to say a prayer for you, Elizabeth," said the man. "I'm going to ask God to bless you with something that will make you very happy."

Elizabeth smiled, and Mary and Matthew were touched by the warmth and simplicity of this man.

Elizabeth knew immediately what blessing would make her happy.

"Thank you," Matthew said. "That's very kind of you."

"I'm grateful to all three of you. May God bless you all."

"Excuse me," Elizabeth said.

The man bent forward toward her. "Yes."

"Can I ask you something?"

"Sure."

"What's it like to be blind?"

Mary and Matthew felt the blood rush into their cheeks.

"Elizabeth, please..." said Mary, but before she had a chance to finish, the man interrupted.

THE MIRACLES

"It's all right," he said softly. "I don't mind."

All were silent for a moment.

The man straightened up and looked directly toward the place where he knew Elizabeth was standing. "Being blind means that -- more than most people -- you get a chance to appreciate the senses that you have that do work, like the sense of smell: I take a deep breath in this crisp December air and I savor it and I am invigorated by it. I smell life and I am grateful for it."

He took a deep breath, inhaling long and hardy, inhaling, inhaling, inhaling, until Elizabeth thought he would burst. Never had anyone in her presence inhaled as deeply as this man at this moment.

"And the sense of hearing: I listen to my radio, I listen to a full orchestra playing a symphony by Beethoven or a piece by Gershwin and I am at once dazzled by the fullness of it and awed by each individual instrument. I'm blessed to be able to discern -- probably better than most sighted people -- the sound of each individual instrument." He paused, as if hearing a favorite piece in full singularity in his head.

"And the sense of taste: even the simplest foods taste delicious -- each and every time. The flavor assaults my tongue and blossoms into the most wonderful sense of satisfaction."

"And the sense of touch: I am blessed with fingers that are sensitive and that speak to

117

me of the things of this world that I'm not able to see."

Mary and Matthew each had their mouths open a bit in awe of this man who had just described his being blind not as an affliction -- as others may have described it -- but as a blessing. His entire description was positive, not negative. They felt blessed to have heard it, and they felt grateful for all that they had been given in their own lives.

"How long have you been blind?" Elizabeth asked.

Once again, Mary was a bit embarrassed at her daughter's innocent question, but before she had a chance to say anything, the man responded.

"Since I was a child," he said. "Probably younger than you. I have faint memories of what the world looks like, but sometimes I wonder if they're real images or just embellishments that my imagination has added through the years."

He paused for a moment, apparently focusing on a particular thought. When he spoke again, the tone of his voice had taken on a sense of yearning that had not been apparent until then. "I'll tell you a little secret," he said.

This thought was touching him deeply. It was apparent. He took a deep breath and sighed.

"Though I'm very grateful for all that I've been given in my life, there are times that I do wish that I could see, times like right now, so that I could see the faces of the lovely little family that has come to my aid."

Elizabeth liked this man. "You said before," she said, "that you were going to say a special prayer for me."

"Yes."

"Were you going to say it now or after I'm gone?"

"I can say it now if you want."

"That would be great."

He felt behind him and when he was sure of his position in relation to the steps, he sat down. He put his hands together and bowed his head. In a moment, he raised it again. "That's it," he said. "I asked God to bless you with something that would make you happy."

Elizabeth climbed up the first step to be a bit closer to him. "Thanks," she said as she touched her hand to his temple near his eye.

Suddenly he straightened his back. His mouth dropped and he was very rigid. He put his hand on the railing and vigorously lifted himself to a standing position. "My God!" he said. "My God!"

Mary and Matthew were startled and leaned toward him for support. They wondered what was wrong.

"Are you all right?" Matthew asked. "What's wrong?"

The man shook his head vigorously. "Wrong? Nothing's wrong." He shook his head again and he began to cry. "Everything is right. Everything is right." He was crying hard now.

Despite his words, his behavior made Mary concerned. "Is there anything we can do?"

The man looked at her. And then at Matthew. And then at Elizabeth. He smiled. "No, there's nothing you can do. I think Elizabeth has done all that can be done."

Matthew and Mary were confused.

The man turned from Elizabeth to them once again. "I can see," he said softly. "I can see your faces. I can see those blue and red cars parked behind you. I can see those brown leaves on the sidewalk. I can see that beautiful pink sky." He was crying more heavily now. "My God, thank you. Thank you." He fell to his knees.

Mary's eyes opened wide at the news and Matthew stayed frozen in place. He looked to his little daughter, still standing atop the first step of the long staircase. She was taking in the joy of this simple, generous man and she was smiling. There was no sign of surprise on her face.

CHAPTER EIGHTEEN

DAY FOUR (Continued)

Matthew stood in the dark of his bedroom, peering through the curtains to the street below. The holiday lights blinked in the windows up and down the street, illuminating more clearly in sporadic bursts the burgeoning assembly of people.

The throng was much more formidable now, no longer composed of journalists only. In the light from the streetlamps, Matthew could see the stanchions that the police had set up to separate the media from the curious visitors. The crowd behind the stanchions seemed to be growing even as he watched. Yet, he knew, it was not nearly as big as it would be by the morning.

He looked at his watch. In 5 minutes he would watch the 10:00 o'clock news. He knew that one of the stories would be about the blind man who could now see, about the modern day Bartimaeus, about the blind man who was touched by God through the hand of a little girl. That was news. Good news.

For a minute, Matthew wished that there could be more stories like that, good news rather than the kind of news that dominated the airwaves. As it was, he was certain that the reports would be exaggerated and sensational, but this story, he knew, was good news and no matter how they dressed it, there was no changing that.

He knew, too, that this particular story would spread fast. The crowd below was witness to that. The story had not yet been printed or aired in the media, yet word-of-mouth had already brought all these people below to a little street in Brooklyn to see what they could see, or hear what they could hear. They were mostly from the neighborhood now, or from bordering neighborhoods. Maybe some had come from Staten Island or Manhattan. But soon, Matthew knew, they would come not only from other boroughs, but also from other states, other countries, other continents.

Once the story had been broadcast on television and radio, and printed in the morning papers, the throng would grow enormously, especially when they learned that Elizabeth had said that the Blessed Virgin would appear again

122

in the morning. People would come from afar to this place. Something special was happening here. A little girl was in touch with heaven and those around her could be blessed like the blind man. They would come.

He looked out at the networks' platforms -- there were three now -- blocking the sidewalk in front of Mrs. Mulrooney's house, the scaffolding laden with cameras and lights and endless supply of thick cables. Colored garland entwined the bars of the scaffolding, indicating that the structures would be here for a long time. 77th Street had been transformed, Matthew thought, from a quiet little street to a media center and to a magnet for the curious, the desperate, the faithful, the worshippers and the tourists.

There was nothing, he concluded, that he or Mary or Elizabeth could have done up to this point to make it any different. Nor should it be different. None of this had been planned. This was just happening, one piece at a time, one piece after the next. This was, apparently, the way that the Blessed Virgin wanted it.

He looked at his watch once more. It was time to go downstairs to watch television. It was time to hear the good news.

Edward F. Droge, Jr.

CHAPTER NINETEEN

DAY FIVE

Randall Prens sat at his office desk, reading the four-star edition of the newspaper. He seemed pleased at the story that he had written for the front page. After a few minutes, he abandoned the paper to engage his computer. There was more to write for tomorrow's edition, much more. A sea of papers and several notepads were spread before him and the early morning sun poured through the window and washed across them.

Bill Dugan, the assignment editor, a crusty looking man with yellowish white hair and a ruddy nose, was glued to his computer screen, reviewing the overnight wire stories, and Elsie, a cleaning woman, leisurely emptied

124

waste baskets that lay in the aisles. No one else was in the office at this hour.

Not usually at the office this early, himself, today Prens had good reason. And as long as he was going to be here, he had committed himself to catch up on a story he was writing. His pace at the keyboard was marked with alternate moments: feverish bursts of clicking one moment, languid pauses of glancing at the screen the next, as a master painter might stop every now and then to look at his work and admire the progress.

Prens had his head down, lost in his story, when he heard Elsie's voice behind him.

"Someone here to see you, Mr. Prens."

He turned to see a petite, white-haired woman approaching his desk. The black frame of her glasses was the most prominent feature of her face. Obviously a senior citizen, she walked with a slight but conspicuous limp.

Prens held out his hand. "I'm glad you were able to make it," he said.

She smiled. "It's right on my way to work. I'm glad *you* were able to come in so early. If I can believe what I pick up on television, I know that reporters usually work in the afternoons and nights."

He nodded politely.

She glanced around at the desks and computers and it was apparent that she was taken with what she saw. "This is my first time in a newspaper office." She giggled like a teenager. "I'm thrilled." She looked around further, her mouth open a bit as if it were the Sphinx or the Great Pyramids she was seeing for the first time. "I've seen them on TV, in the movies, and in the theater, but I never stepped foot in a real newspaper office before now."

Prens did not see it as a big deal but he humored her. "Feel free to walk around before you leave."

That obviously pleased her. "Oh, thanks. I certainly will."

"I'm trying to meet a deadline here," he said, gesturing to his computer screen, "or I'd show you around personally." He wondered if she could detect his insincerity. He had plenty of time before the deadline.

She nodded as if she understood his problem and was sympathetic.

He rolled a swivel chair from the adjacent desk nearer to his own desk and he offered her a seat. For the next half hour they talked, with Prens having more to say than the woman.

When she rose from her chair, he did as well. He took his wallet from a back pocket, fished around for a few seconds, and handed her some bills. She smiled, extended her hand for a shake, and limped off on her personal exploration of the office.

Prens watched her for only a moment before sitting back down to his computer. Before his first clicks, however, a smirk grew slowly across his lips.

CHAPTER TWENTY

DAY FIVE (Continued)

Matthew opened his front door and reached down to the stoop to retrieve the morning newspaper. Without warning, cameras flashed and shouts came at him to look up so that they could get a clear shot of his face.

He looked out. He was shocked to see hundreds of people -- maybe thousands, he was not that good at estimating -- in front of his house at this early hour. The cameras flashed more vigorously now as he faced them. The assembly of journalists in front of the house was bigger than it had been the day before, as was, most conspicuously, the crowd of onlookers behind the stanchions, who strained to get a glimpse at what all the fuss was about in the doorway.

Matthew felt awkward, standing in his pajamas in front of all these people, all of whom seemed to be either gaping at him or taking his picture. He sighed. All he wanted to do was get the newspaper, and the huge crowd made an event out of it.

There were so many people. And it seemed so early -- he had not even eaten breakfast yet. Were they here all night, he wondered. He re-assessed the number: it was definitely more than a thousand. Much more. He wondered if there could actually be two thousand people in front of his house. Or three thousand. At this hour?

He shook his head. Why not, he thought. They came to see Our Lady.

He retrieved the paper and hustled back inside, closing the door quickly, as much to escape the attention as to keep out the cold. He leaned against the door for a moment to catch his breath.

Calmed, he sat at the kitchen table with a cup of coffee that had already been poured and he unfurled the newspaper. He did not have to search very hard to find the article he knew would be there on the front page. There it was, there on the bottom right hand side, the large-lettered headline: "Miracle in Brooklyn? Blind Man Sees." In smaller letters underneath it read: "Little 'Apparition' Girl Present." And underneath that: "by Randall Prens."

THE MIRACLES

He read the story. He knew the details, but he wanted to see how it would be presented in the paper. The blind man was quoted several times. Understandably, he was extremely grateful. He thanked the little girl for her part, but made it clear that it was the work of God. Matthew felt good for that.

It seemed to Matthew that Prens, though good with the facts, had written the story with much skepticism. Though he did not come right out and say it, the reporter made it seem as if the readers should not be surprised to discover ultimately that this was all a grand hoax of some sort.

Nevertheless, the story was fairly accurate and informative. Reading on, Matthew learned that apparently the blind man had not known of the apparition involving Elizabeth, and, when informed of it, he said that it only reinforced his sense that she had served as God's vehicle to restore his sight.

More than once in the article, Prens alluded to the New Testament story of Bartimaeus, the blind man who was cured by Jesus. According to Mark's gospel, Jesus remarked on the faith of the blind man and declared it responsible for his healing.

Matthew's attention flicked from the paper to the movement he caught from the corner of his eye. With Fluffy cradled in one arm, Elizabeth was coming down the stairs in her flannel pajamas, her sleepers, the ones with

129

the feet on them. She joined him at the kitchen table.

"Good morning, sweetie," he said. "It's a bit early for you, isn't it?"

"Hi, Daddy. I couldn't get back to sleep."

"Back to sleep? When did you wake up?"

"A while ago. When..." She hesitated for just a moment, but long enough to signal to him that she had second thoughts of saying it. "...when Our Lady spoke to me this morning."

Matthew put down the paper. "Did she appear to you?"

"No. I didn't see her. But I woke up to her voice, talking softly to me, as if she were right there with me by my bed."

He leaned across the table to get closer to her. "And what did she say?"

"She said she'd see me at ten o'clock this morning."

"Ten o'clock?"

She nodded.

"So that's the time she will appear to you?"

"I guess so."

"Did she say anything else?"

"She said that I'd have to be strong because there would be many thousands of people outside today, but that it would be okay because she would be with me."

THE MIRACLES

Matthew nodded. He would not doubt that there would be many thousands of onlookers outside of their house today.

"Anything else?"

"Just that that was what she wanted -- to have as many people as possible to hear her message."

"What message?"

Elizabeth shrugged her shoulders. "I don't know."

"Anything else?"

She shook her head.

Matthew put his hand on top of hers as it lay on the table. He smiled. "I'll be there with you, too," he said.

She smiled back.

Mary, in her bathrobe and slippers, came down the stairs and joined them at the table.

"Well, aren't we up early," she sighed lightly.

Elizabeth gave her a hug and Matthew offered a peck on the lips.

"Elizabeth says she heard Our Lady's voice this morning," Matthew said.

Mary opened her eyes a bit wider at that.

Matthew continued: "Apparently she will visit her at ten o'clock this morning."

Mary looked at her daughter. "Did she specifically say ten o'clock?"

Elizabeth nodded. "Yes."

"Are you sure you weren't dreaming?"

"I'm sure."

Matthew spoke up once again: "And Our Lady wants as many people outside as possible."

Elizabeth anticipated her mother's question of confirmation and, without Mary having to say anything, the little girl nodded again, as if to say "yes, I'm sure I wasn't dreaming."

"We should probably let the media know the time," Matthew said. "It would be best if people knew a specific time."

Mary agreed.

Matthew took his robe from the back of the chair and put it on over his pajamas. "I'll tell them right now." He walked to the front door and went out. Before he closed the door, Mary and Elizabeth could see the flashes from several cameras.

In a few minutes, Matthew was back. "They were glad to hear it," he said, taking off his robe and slinging it back over his chair. "Apparently, the networks will mention it in their morning shows. I'm sure there will be a good crowd here for Our Lady when she comes."

He nestled back into his place at the table and, as best they could, the three of them tried to have an uneventful breakfast.

CHAPTER TWENTY-ONE

DAY FIVE (Continued)

Neither Matthew, nor Mary, nor Elizabeth could have imagined the size of the crowd outside their house at nine-forty-five. As the three of them peered from the upstairs bedroom window, they could only gasp. A sea of faces, thousands upon thousands of faces, old and young, different colors, different sizes, different shapes, stared up at them from the street below. Many present were in wheelchairs or on crutches.

People stretched up and down 77th Street for as far as the eye could see, well beyond 5th Avenue on one end and well beyond 6th Avenue on the other. Not only were the sidewalks and roadways overflowing, but the rooftops and the windows and the yards and the tops of the parked cars -- every available space that could hold a person was occupied.

Elizabeth, with Fluffy tucked safely under one arm, was smiling. "Our Lady will be pleased."

Matthew looked at his watch. It was time. He had agreed to a brief press conference to permit a few questions before ten o'clock.

"We're not being very good hosts," Mary said. "We've left poor Father Dunne downstairs by himself."

They filed out of the room and went downstairs to join the priest. His gray hair neatly parted, his spectacles balanced gently on the tip of his nose, he was sitting calmly at the kitchen table, enjoying a cup of coffee.

"Forgive us, Father," Mary said, blushing. "We've been looking at the crowd from the upstairs window, and it's enormous."

"They said on the radio this morning," said the priest, "that apparitions at Fatima and Lourdes and Medjugorje attracted crowds in the tens of thousands."

Matthew shook his head in amazement and awe. He stooped down to little Elizabeth, today with a pony tail, a light blue sweater and a navy skirt. White stockings would protect her from the December chill. He looked directly into her eyes. "Are you ready for this?"

"Sure, Daddy," she said without hesitation and with no apparent sign of anxiety. What she was about to face seemed about as

daunting to her as the prospect of taking a ride
on a swing. "I'm not afraid. Our Lady said that
the crowd would be big and that she'd be with
me."

Elizabeth put Fluffy down on the sofa.
Her cat, she said, was not ready for all the
attention and would stay inside this morning.
From her pocket, she took out a simple black
rosary. A silver tag that said "Elizabeth" was
tied to the chain below the cross. "Mommy
gave me this rosary," she said. "I'm going to
keep it with me."

Matthew smiled. He was so proud of
his little girl.

Father Dunne approached Elizabeth, put
his hand on her shoulder, and whispered a
blessing as he made the sign of the cross in the
air above her head.

They all took a deep breath at the door,
and went out. Cameras flashed furiously and
the photographers from all sides shouted at
once to them -- especially Elizabeth -- to face
them so that they could get the best angle. A
bank of bright lights on each of the three
platforms erected across the street switched on
almost simultaneously and the light washed
across the front stoop.

A loud cheer went up from the crowd
and they applauded enthusiastically. Many held
up signs and banners, citing the Bible, praising
God, and acknowledging Elizabeth.

Elizabeth, squinting from the lights,
unable to see the signs, was between her

parents, holding their hands, and Mary and Matthew both squeezed her a bit to offer her comfort as they made their way to the set of microphones on the table at the bottom of the steps. Father Dunne followed them down the stairs and, like a good soldier, stood behind them at the table.

Dozens of police officers ringed the table, and stanchions kept the journalists at a distance. The crowd of onlookers could get no closer than the middle of the street, which had been closed to traffic. When Mary, Matthew and Elizabeth were seated, the crowd quieted quickly.

When Matthew had agreed to the press conference, he had insisted that there be some order, rather than dozens of questions being asked by dozens of different reporters all at once. He had asked that the reporters themselves determine the order in which they would take turns, but that only one question at a time be asked.

One of the women reporters was first: "I wonder," she said, "if Elizabeth can help us to understand why those of us present yesterday were able to see the light, yet the cameras were not able to record it."

Elizabeth shook her head. "I only know..." She stopped, startled at the booming volume of her voice. She had not been prepared for the public address system hooked up by the media to permit all present, even the tens of thousands in the crowd that stretched to the avenues, to hear what she had to say. The volume level on the system was turned up very high.

Recovering quickly, she continued: "I only know that Our Lady said that others would know that she was present, but that I was the only one who could see her."

A male reporter spoke up: "Why is she appearing here?"

"I don't know for sure. Maybe she'll tell me this morning."

Another woman reporter took her turn: "Can you tell us a little about..."

Before she had a chance to finish her question, however, Elizabeth rose from the table and looked up to the sky. She knelt and took out her rosary.

At that moment, the bright light with rays of gold appeared in the sky. Its golden rays shot from its periphery in every direction like some magnificent display of fireworks. But no display of fireworks made by mankind could be this bright, particularly in the daylight

The bright light descended slowly from the heavens and came to rest a few feet above Elizabeth's head. Its intensity, many times the intensity of the lights from the platforms, forced all eyes away from it, except for the little girl's. Mary and Matthew and Father Dunne all knelt near the table.

A loud reaction of surprise and awe went up from the crowd at the appearance of the light, and immediately the vast majority dropped to their knees and blessed themselves with the sign of the cross. Most in the assembly of journalists, closer to the light, also knelt. All of the policemen were on their knees. Most all present held their hands to their face to shield their eyes from the intense brightness.

Elizabeth, though, was looking up directly at the light and she was smiling. Her big brown eyes were wide open and her lips were moving as though she were talking, but no one near her could hear words coming from her mouth. She held her rosary firmly.

Cameras flashed and videos rolled. There was much activity on each of the platforms across the street, news anchors speaking softly into their microphones, describing what they were seeing, cameramen covering their lenses with filters for the light, tech people checking their equipment to be certain that it was working properly.

The crowd was deathly silent. Tens of thousands of people, as far as the eye could see, and not a word could be heard from them.

Elizabeth stayed kneeling and smiling and speaking to the bright light for several minutes. Five minutes passed. Ten minutes.

Suddenly, somewhere from the depths of the crowd, far back toward 5th Avenue, a woman began to sing the hymn, "Hail, Holy Queen." Quickly a few voices joined her. And then a few more, and a few more, and a few more, until, as a fire spreading swiftly through dry brush, virtually the entire throng was ignited and singing along, caught up in the moment, praising their Holy Queen.

The cameras on the platforms and in the assembly of journalists below swept the crowd to capture the event. This was very very special. Everyone knew it, not just the media. All present knew that this was a special moment in their lives, a moment that they would never forget, a moment that they would treasure beyond things material.

Most kneeling, many in wheelchairs or on crutches, some joining hands with strangers beside them, tens of thousands of visitors to this obscure little street in an often maligned borough of New York City, rang out a hymn of praise to the Mother of Jesus, who graced them with her presence this December morning. Later, the newscasts would report that the song could be heard as far away as Wall Street in Manhattan, many miles in the distance, and that, in fact, the usual din of lower Manhattan was quieted for several minutes as people stopped in awe and appreciation to listen to the heavenly hymn.

Elizabeth was still focused on the light, virtually oblivious to the music, when, suddenly, seemingly from nowhere, a sparrow flew on to her shoulder. The little girl did not flinch. From there the sparrow jumped to Elizabeth's hands. As if wanting to cooperate, she held her rosary exposed. The silver tag that said "Elizabeth" contrasted with the blackness of the

beads. The sparrow bent to the rosary, picked
it up in its beak, and flew into the clear blue sky.

All who could see the bird were riveted
to it as it ascended. The cameras and the
videotapes swiveled skyward in pursuit. Higher
and higher the sparrow flew, its wings flapping
vigorously, the simple black rosary dangling
from its beak, until, eventually, the bird was no
longer visible. The crowd buzzed with
excitement as the story spread quickly among
them for the benefit of those who were not able
to see it.

Twelve minutes had passed from the
first appearance of the light, and Elizabeth was
still kneeling, still smiling, still looking up and
moving her lips. Then, however, she closed her
eyes and bowed her head. The light began to
rise slowly into the sky. Every camera present
followed it as it ascended, and in a moment it
was gone.

The crowd began to come to life as
many rose from their kneeling position and the
platforms stayed bustling with activity. Little
Elizabeth, however, remained kneeling, praying,
eyes closed. Mary and Matthew and Father
Dunne stayed on their knees as well, as did
several of the policemen and many of the
journalists.

After a few minutes, Elizabeth opened
her eyes and turned, smiling, to her mother and
father. They smiled back. She joined them and
they hugged.

THE MIRACLES

"Our Lady wants me to deliver her message," she said.

Mary and Matthew nodded in understanding and led her to the table. They remained standing behind her. The journalists tried their best to be poised and patient as it took a few minutes for the crowd to quiet, but the events of the past few minutes had ruffled even the crustiest of veterans among them.

Sensing that it was orderly enough and that the public address system would permit all to hear her, Elizabeth leaned forward into the cluster of microphones before her at the table. Her voice boomed into the air. "That was the Blessed Virgin again."

When she said it, many of the journalists smiled at her innocence. Yes, they had suspected it was.

"She wants me to tell you what she said. I know that I'm not able to remember everything, but she said that she would help me, and so I might have to go slowly at times."

The media was at once awed by the poise of this little six-year-old and ravenous for the news that she would momentarily provide them. Every pen was poised, every camera pointed, and every microphone checked.

Elizabeth's hands were together on the table, as if she were praying. She swallowed hard, took a deep breath, and began. "Just as Our Lady said yesterday, she wants us to pray to her son, Jesus. She wants us to ask for his forgiveness and for his help. She mentioned moral decay again and said that each of you knows in your heart that what is happening in the world is wrong and needs to be corrected."

She closed her eyes, as if calling on the Blessed Virgin for help in remembering what else was said. In just a few seconds she opened them and continued. "She said she is appearing here because she knows that it will be noticed and she wants as many people as possible to hear her message and to know that she is with us. She said that she is the mother of all, not just of Catholics or Christians, but of all religions and all beliefs. And she said that she feels the pains of a mother for her children. She said that her message is for all of her children. She cares about all of us and Jesus cares about all of us. They want us to be good and to love each other."

Again Elizabeth closed her eyes, as if drawing on divine intervention to help her memory, and again in only a matter of seconds she was ready to continue. It was obvious to those listening to her that this little six-year-old was speaking well above her years, and most in the crowd believed that she, indeed, was receiving divine help in relaying this message.

"Our Lady asks each one of us to make an individual decision to be holy. She wants us to pray to Jesus for help and she says that he will listen to our prayers. When Jesus comes again -- and we have to be prepared for that, because it could happen at anytime -- when Jesus comes again, every man, woman, and child will view their own souls as God does, and will know their own status. It will be too late to change it then, and, so, Jesus wants us to follow his ways now."

Once more she closed her eyes for a few seconds and then opened them and resumed: "The Blessed Virgin also said that she's appearing because she wants us to know that her son has not given up on us. She wants us to have hope. And she wants us to convert and to be true to him."

She closed her eyes and this time it was longer than a few seconds and she had not yet opened them. The journalists wondered if she were finished, but after a minute or so she opened them again.

"She said that you won't be able to see her and your cameras won't be able to capture her light because she wants to give you a chance to practice your faith. You are blessed, she said, when you believe even though you can't see. She said she's appearing to me because I'm six and many of you will believe me for that very reason -- because I'm six. She said that many of you will believe a child more than you will believe a grown-up."

She paused, this time without closing her eyes. "She said that some still wouldn't believe that she was here. It's important that the world hears her message, though, and because of that she said she would give the world a sign. It will be tomorrow. She didn't say what it would be, except that it would be easy to see that it was a sign from her."

As soon as Elizabeth was finished the journalists fired questions at her fast and furiously, all at once, so much so that hardly a single question was able to be understood. Matthew shook his head. He had told the media representatives that this was exactly the kind of scene that he had wanted to avoid.

Randall Prens jumped out from the stanchions and turned to face his colleagues. He raised his hands to quiet them down. One by one they followed his direction, until, after only a minute, the full assembly had grown silent.

"We made a commitment here," said Prens, "and, as you can see, if we don't abide by it we're not going to get very far. If we can just go back to asking questions one at a time in the predetermined order, I think we'll all be happy."

There were nods and mumbles of assent. Speaking up was the woman reporter who was in the middle of asking a question earlier when the light descended. "It was my turn, as you recall."

Prens acknowledged her, and stepped back behind the stanchion.

The woman addressed herself to Elizabeth: "You said yesterday that the Blessed Virgin Mary was beautiful, more beautiful than any picture of her, but can you tell us what she's wearing and what she's doing -- like standing, kneeling or what?"

THE MIRACLES

Elizabeth did not hesitate. "She *is* beautiful, and her clothes are as bright as the sun. And there's a light around her head, almost like a halo, a bright light with stars, and it makes her face more beautiful than any face I've ever seen. What was the other question -- oh, yes -- what is she doing...well, she's standing, facing me, with her hands together like this..." She put her hands together, as if in prayer. "...and she speaks with me and then we pray."

Every journalist present was riveted to each word of this little girl.

Randall Prens was next to ask a question. He gestured to the huge crowd behind him, a crowd that was bursting at the seams and that was intensely listening to the questions and answers as they were being broadcast over the public address system. "As probably you've noticed, many of those who are here today are in wheelchairs or have braces or crutches or are afflicted in some other way. If I understand it correctly, you've worked it out with the police department to set up the stanchions in a little while to permit the people to pass by your house in some orderly fashion. I'm wondering what you plan to do as they pass. Is this intended to be a kind of healing procession, and are you claiming that those who are afflicted and who pass by will be healed, as the blind man allegedly was healed yesterday?"

Elizabeth looked up to her father. Matthew, having noted the slight emphasis that Prens had placed on the word "allegedly," leaned into the cluster of microphones to respond for his daughter. "This set up was arranged in response to the hundreds and hundreds of requests that were passed along to us. Apparently this is what the people want. We certainly don't make any claims about what will happen. It's simply a way for the people and Elizabeth to exchange greetings. Elizabeth will pray for them all. If anyone is healed, that's great, but it'll be God's will that determines it."

Elizabeth whispered into her father's ear: "I'm going to like saying hello to the people, Daddy." He smiled at her.

Prens was pleased and the corners of his mouth turned up as the next journalist took a turn with a question.

CHAPTER TWENTY-TWO

DAY FIVE (Continued)

Mary bustled around the kitchen, checking the cake in the oven, mixing the chocolate frosting in a bowl, checking the refrigerator to see that there was enough milk. Though the house was not excessively warm, beads of perspiration dotted her brow from the hectic pace she forced upon herself. She felt she had to hurry. She wanted to be sure to be finished by the time Elizabeth came in.

She glimpsed out the window and saw the line of people as they filed past Elizabeth in front of the house. Elizabeth smiled at each one and each one smiled back. Some reached out to touch her, but the police officers standing by the stanchions were vigilant and careful not to let anyone get too tight a grip. Matthew, too, standing beside her, was watchful.

Just going by as Mary looked out was a little white-haired lady with a conspicuous limp. The black frame of her glasses attracted Mary's attention. Elizabeth held her hand out and the woman was able to touch it. Her eyes said that she was very grateful for having done so.

One by one they filed past, most walking, many in wheelchairs, some with braces or crutches. All had come to see the child who had been touched by the Blessed Virgin. Most had faith in their eyes, but many had desperation.

From her kitchen window, Mary could not see the end of the line, but she hoped that it would not be much longer before Elizabeth and Matthew came in. It was nearly one o'clock and they had not eaten since breakfast.

Mary knew that Elizabeth wanted to accommodate all who had come to see her -- some from far distances -- but both Mary and Matthew had told her that that might not be possible. Mary had heard on the radio that someone had estimated that more than thirty thousand people had travelled to 77th Street to witness the apparition and to see and hear the little girl, Elizabeth.

Thirty thousand people would take a long time to file by. Just how long, however, Mary did not know. She glanced across the street at the platforms. The faces had changed, but still a full complement of television people busied themselves above the crowd. Mary knew that there would be media present throughout the day and night. And, as full as the streets were, she knew that they would swell even more with each apparition.

She pulled the cake from the oven and set it on the counter. She would let it sit for a while and then frost it.

If they were not in by the time she was finished, she would call them.

As the cake sat cooling, she moved to the living room. From a plastic bag on the coffee table, she took a roll of crepe and began to hang streamers across the archways and up the railing of the stairs near the Christmas tree. It took only a few minutes to unfurl three rolls. She took a step back and admired the job she had done. Streamers were everywhere and it certainly looked festive.

That completed, she took from the plastic bag a package of balloons and began to blow them up. Red, green, blue, yellow, each was a vibrant color. She smiled. It was fun to try to make her little daughter happy, and she knew that her labor would bear fruit in just a little while.

CHAPTER TWENTY-THREE

DAY FIVE (Continued)

Randall Prens padded his loafers along the carpet of the newspaper office and stalled outside the glass door that said "Henry Weintraub." His editor was on the phone and Prens knew better than to enter until he was off.

As surreptitiously as he could, head down, glancing every now and then from the corner of his eye, Prens studied Weintraub as he spoke. He noted the editor's horseshoe of white hair atop his head and Ben Franklin glasses on the tip of his nose. This was the textbook look for an editor, Prens thought. This was the way he wanted to look when he was an editor.

Weintraub hung up and motioned Prens into the office. The editor shuffled some papers out of the way, and then devoted his undivided attention to his reporter.

"What happened this morning?" Weintraub asked.

"It was pretty much the same as yesterday, except it lasted a little longer. It's incredible how this light appears, surrounded by golden rays that undulate and rotate. It seems unearthly, and it's intensely bright, too bright for anyone to look at directly -- except the little girl. She's able to look right into the light with no problem, smiling and praying."

"How about the light? Did we get the light on film this time?"

Prens shook his head. "Nope. And I checked with a couple of my contacts in television and they tell me that it didn't come out on video either. It's the strangest thing. It's so bright that, if anything, you'd think it would white-out the film or the video, but, instead, everything shows up as clear as can be as if the light weren't even there. No one can figure it out."

Now Weintraub took a turn shaking his head. "It defies the laws of nature."

Prens nodded. "Maybe that's the point."

Weintraub shrugged his shoulders. "Any new twists on the story?" he asked.

Prens took a seat near the glass door. "Well, two new twists at this point. The little girl embellished on the message she claims the lady is giving to her -- and let me say that this little one has become quite the darling of the media who are present; she's a charmer and she speaks more like a Yale graduate than a little six-year-old with a ponytail -- but, anyhow, the add-on today was that the lady has promised a sign for the world, to demonstrate to all that she is, in fact, appearing as the little girl claims."

"What kind of a sign?"

"She didn't say."

"When is it supposed to take place?"

"Tomorrow."

"You're planning to be there, I assume."

"I wouldn't miss it."

"You said two twists. What's the other?"

"The elderly woman I told you about, the one with arthritis and osteoporosis."

"Oh, right. She was going to be there today?"

Prens nodded. "I had hoped that she would be able to get to talk with the little Depaul girl in private, but there had to be thirty or forty thousand people there today. The set-up was arranged as a walk-by."

"And, so, your woman is going to come back here afterward and confirm that there was no miraculous cure."

"Exactly. She's coming here later this afternoon."

"Okay. Write it as you see it."

"Just the facts," said Prens. "Just the facts." He smiled.

CHAPTER TWENTY-FOUR

DAY FIVE (Continued)

Mary looked at the kitchen clock: it was three-fifteen. She went to the window one more time to check on Elizabeth and Matthew. They still had not been in for lunch. She had decided to go out to get them. If they stayed out much longer, they would faint: they had not eaten nor taken a break since the morning.

She peered through the curtain and saw the line filing past Elizabeth. It seemed as formidable a line as it had been all day. Mary came to the realization an hour ago that it would stay formidable. Not only was the crowd ever growing, but, Mary was certain, many had filed past on the line more than once.

She came from the window and turned
her attention to the chocolate cake on the
counter near the stove. She took a knife and,
like an artist putting the finishing touches on her
masterpiece, she dabbed the frosting three, four,
five more times to get the exact look that she
wanted. She brought the cake to the table and
placed it in the center. From a box lying
nearby, she took little pink candles and plunged
them into the chocolate frosting around the
outside of the cake. She checked the table
settings and was satisfied that all was in order.

She looked up from the table to check
the house. She was pleased at what she saw.
The crepe was strung festively, the balloons
added color, and the lights on the Christmas
tree gave the living room just the right feel.
This was definitely a celebratory environment.

She slipped her apron over her head and
went to the window one last time. No matter
what the status was, she was intent on going
outside to call them in. But, to her delight,
Matthew and Elizabeth were walking up the
stairs. She hurried to the door to meet them.

The door opened and Elizabeth stepped
inside. Her eyes opened wide at the
decorations. Matthew, close behind, winked at
Mary and together they both yelled "Surprise!"

"Happy Birthday," Mary said. "Just a
little late."

Elizabeth was wearing a giant smile.
"Wow," was all she could manage.

THE MIRACLES

Matthew lifted his little girl up. "You didn't think we'd forget, did you?"

Mary motioned them into the living room. Matthew set Elizabeth down and her eyes got wider still when she spied on the sofa several gifts, wrapped neatly and tied with fancy ribbons.

"Before you open them..." Mary said, scurrying to the Christmas tree and retrieving the rectangular box from underneath, wrapped in blue foil with a white bow in the corner, "...open this." She handed the box to her daughter.

Elizabeth tore open the foil and opened the box quickly. Her eyes gleamed and her mouth dropped when she saw the decorative, majestic angel, handsomely carved from light wood, and painted masterfully with simple pastels. It was casting its stern glance downward. Its wings were spread far from its body and its hands were raised to the side, as if offering counsel and protection.

Matthew was pleased with Elizabeth's reaction. "I hope that's the kind of angel you wanted for the top of the tree."

"Oh, yes, Daddy. This is just perfect." She did note how stern the angel's face was and felt just for a moment that she wished he looked happier, but she would never mention it aloud. She convinced herself that it was probably better that the angel had a stern look, in order to keep his mind on the business of protecting them.

155

Matthew took hold of her waist, carried her to the Christmas tree, and hoisted her up. She slid the tube at the bottom of the angel over the top branch. Matthew took a step back and as Mary joined them, they stood there for a moment, admiring their guardian angel.

"Now," Mary said, "the sooner you get these other presents open, the sooner we can all have some chocolate cake."

Elizabeth, still in her father's arms, reached toward her mother and the three of them had a family hug in the middle of the living room. The guardian angel stared sternly from his perch atop the tree.

CHAPTER TWENTY-FIVE

DAY FIVE (Continued)

The newspaper office bustled with the activity of a lively news day. Graphic artists shuffled in and out with their art, copy editors stared at their computer screens and scrolled the day's stories before their eyes, and reporters, with telephones cradled on their shoulders, ate their sandwiches with one hand and clicked at their keyboards with the other.

The tubular fluorescent bulbs that stretched across the ceiling from one end of the wide office to the other washed the rows of adjacent desks and cubicles below with enough kilowatts worth of light to make all present unmindful that the sun had set an hour earlier and that outside the building it was dark.

Randall Prens, his tie pulled away from his collar, sat clicking at his keyboard and watching the results appear on the monitor in front of him when the phone rang. He picked it up.

"Prens," he said perfunctorily. He listened for a moment, and then said "Right. Send her up."

He hung up the phone in one swift motion and continued typing, trying hard not to skip a beat. Instinctively, when he felt that enough time had passed for his visitor to have taken the elevator to the third floor and to have walked through the labyrinth of hallways and offices outside the news room, he glanced over his shoulder.

Sure enough, the petite white-haired lady with the black framed glasses was just entering the door and turning toward him. He was pleased with himself at how good he was getting at his little game of estimating time.

As the little woman walked toward him, he knew there was something different about her, but it took him a minute to figure out what it was. His jaw dropped just a bit at the realization that she was not walking with a limp. It had been so conspicuous this morning, and now there was no hint of it as she strode with a very lively gait, a gait that would be the envy of many a woman her age.

She extended her hand for a shake. "Good evening, Mr. Prens."

"Good..." He was not able to finish before she cut him off.

"Have *I* got a story for you." Her face said that this was news, real news.

Prens was intrigued.

"First," she said, fishing out a piece of paper from her pocketbook, "here's your receipt for my visit to the doctor. Thank you -- or, I guess it would be more appropriate to thank the newspaper -- for paying for it."

Prens took the receipt and tossed it on his desk, already cluttered with papers and notepads. "We're glad to do it," he said. "And what did the doctor have to say?"

"Well, that's your story." She was eyeing the chair near his desk. "May I?"

"Sure," he said, pulling the chair closer and motioning her into it. He sat down in his own chair and faced her.

She was bubbling and twitching with excitement. "I went to the apparition, just as we agreed. In fact, I saw you there, but I thought it best not to say hello."

She lowered her head and her voice, and she leaned toward him, as if she were "Deep Throat," talking about the information that would unseat a president. "You know what I mean," she said.

Prens humored her with a nod.

"I couldn't get very close. In fact, I was in the middle of the block and I felt lucky to get there. I was able to stake a spot next to a streetlight, though, and every now and then I climbed up on to the base of it and it got me just high enough to see over most of the heads in the crowd. I could actually see the little girl and the light."

Prens was taking notes and nodding steadily as she talked, encouraging her to provide as much detail as possible. "Did you get to speak to the Depaul girl at all?"

The woman shook her head. "No, I couldn't get to talk with her -- no one could, really, but she did stand in front of her house and people lined up to walk past her. When I walked past her I was filled with a warmth, a spirit of..." She could not find the right word.

Through her black-framed glasses, Prens noticed tears forming in the corner of her eyes. Clearly she had been significantly affected by this experience.

Her face said that she had found the thought she was looking for. "...I was filled with the spirit of God."

"Did she say anything to you?"

"No. She didn't have to, really. She smiled at me, and I was able to reach out and touch her hand as I passed. It was when I touched her hand that I felt as if, through her, I was being touched by God." The tears were streaking her cheeks now and she took a tissue from her pocketbook to wipe them.

Prens was surprised at the details of her story. But the important part for him was the medical angle. "And so you went to the doctor afterward?"

THE MIRACLES

"Yes. I had made an appointment and he examined me thoroughly and I had x-rays and -- I'm not sure if I've got this right -- an M-R-I?" She looked to the reporter for confirmation.

Prens nodded. "M-R-I. Right. I think it stands for Magnetic Resonance Imaging, or something like that. It's a step or two up from an x-ray."

Now she nodded. "That's what the doctor said to me. Well, anyway, I had an M-R-I and the results are your story."

His eyes were open wide and he leaned in when she paused, anxious to hear what she had to say. "And what were those results?"

She took a deep breath. It still was difficult for her to believe it. "My arthritis and my osteoporosis are gone."

"Gone?"

"Completely. It's almost as if they were never there to begin with. My doctor couldn't believe it either. He went back through my files and read his own notes and examined my x-rays and test results. There's no question that I had a classic case of rheumatoid arthritis in my hip -- it's as clear as can be in my file, the x-rays and the tests make it absolutely clear. But now the new x-rays and the M-R-I results show nothing. Absolutely nothing. And I feel great. I know there's nothing there anymore."

Prens was staring incredulously at her, his mouth open, his eyes wide. He ran his fingers through his thick blonde hair. "This is unbelievable."

"That's what I said. You may not have gotten the story you thought you were going to get, but this sure is a story, isn't it?"

He was thinking hard. She was right. This certainly was not the story he had anticipated. In fact, having anticipated that the woman would have had no change whatsoever -- and that fact verified by a doctor -- he had already written much of the story with that angle. It was in his computer. Now, if he was going to go with it, he would have to overhaul it completely. In fact, he would have to start all over again.

She noticed that the corners of his mouth were turned down. "You look disappointed," she said.

"Do I?" He was not aware that it was showing. "No, not disappointed, just surprised. This, after all, is quite a fantastic story." He glanced at the receipt from the doctor. It looked legitimate. He would have to verify all of this, but ostensibly she was a reliable witness whether he liked it or not.

"Fantastic," she said. "That's exactly how I feel. I haven't been able to walk with such spring in my step for years, no, for decades." She was smiling broadly. "That little girl is very special. She's been blessed by God, and, now, so have I."

Prens stood up, and she followed his lead. "Thanks," he said. "I have all I need for now." He held up his notepad, upon which he had written several pages worth of details. "I have your number. If I need to speak with you, I'll call, if that's all right."

"Sure," she said. "To be honest, when I left here this morning, I didn't think I was going to have much news to report to you. But, as long as you were paying for the doctor's visit, I figured I couldn't lose. It was getting near time for a check-up, anyway. I thought I'd get my exam and he would tell me that nothing had changed."

He started walking with her toward the door.

"But this," she said. "Well, this is nothing short of a miracle."

He nodded, though he did not believe in miracles. He stuck his hand out for a shake. "I'll be in touch."

"Thanks. If you hadn't asked me to go there today, I'm sure I wouldn't have. Thanks to you and to your newspaper." She turned and walked with vigor out the door.

Prens walked slowly back to his desk, reviewing the details in his mind, pulling together his thoughts. It did sound like a miracle, didn't it, he thought. But he reminded himself once more: he did not believe in miracles.

He sat and pulled up the story he had written in his computer. As he scrolled it up the screen, he shook his head. He had anticipated incorrectly. The story he had written was awaiting details that he simply could not furnish now.

He glanced around to his editor's office. Weintraub was busy at his desk. Prens got up and walked over slowly.

Weintraub, his Ben Franklin glasses balanced on the tip of his nose, looked up when he felt someone present. "What's up?" he asked.

Prens had his hands in his pocket and, by design, wore a concerned expression. "About the apparition story. That elderly woman angle isn't going to work."

"Why not?"

"She's proven unreliable. I can't trust her as a source."

Weintraub's face said that he wanted more information, but Prens did not volunteer it. The editor let it pass. If a reporter could not feel a source was reliable, it was good enough for him. He did not need to know the details. He shrugged his shoulders. "Write what you've got," he said and he put his head down to get back into his work, signalling Prens that there was no need for further conversation.

"Right." Prens turned and walked back toward his desk. He still had plenty of material from the day's events on 77th Street to give him a story. He did not believe in miracles and he was not about to write a story that gave any indication that he did.

THE MIRACLES

CHAPTER TWENTY-SIX

DAY SIX

Matthew sipped his coffee at the kitchen table and turned to the inside of the newspaper to continue the story that had begun on the first page. Randall Prens was a good writer, he thought, but it was clear that he was skeptical. Though Matthew knew that reporters in general were known to be a cynical lot, he wondered how anyone who had been present for the apparitions and who had seen and heard all that transpired could be so openly skeptical. It was not fair to the readers, Matthew thought: it was not good reporting to weave such doubt so conspicuously through the story.

Elizabeth and Mary coming down the stairs interrupted him and he put the paper down. It was just as well that he did not read any more of that particular story by that particular reporter anyhow, he thought. He refused to allow it to upset him any more than it had.

"Hi, Daddy," Elizabeth said. Her bangs and pigtails bounced as she bounded down the last few stairs.

Matthew admired her yellow top and yellow pants. "You look as bright as the sun this morning, sweetie."

She smiled and gave him a hug.

"Have you seen the crowd?" Mary asked.

Matthew nodded. "They said on the radio that there would probably be more people here today than there was yesterday."

Mary shook her head. "It's hard to believe that 77th Street can hold more people." A new thought made her smile. "But, then, that's what Our Lady said she wanted...right, Elizabeth?"

Elizabeth turned her big brown eyes to her mother. "Our Lady said she wants the whole world to hear her message, Mommy."

"That's a tall order" Matthew said.

"Our Lady will find a way," Elizabeth said with confidence. "Our Lady will find a way."

*   *   *   *   *

166

THE MIRACLES

In the late afternoon sun, tens of
thousands of people, standing elbow to elbow,
peaceful, reverent, calm in this confined space,
prayed in one voice, una voce, in the Vatican
square of St. Peter's Basilica, the largest church
in Christendom. The huge dome of the basilica,
a golden cross at the very top, rose majestically
behind the balcony where the Pope stood,
shepherding his flock, praying with them,
offering them words of encouragement in this
advent of the most holy of celebrations, the
birth of Jesus, their Savior.

From the square the people looked up to
the Vicar of Christ, dressed in white, framed
between two stone columns supporting the
balcony. From the balcony hung a huge red
banner that flapped slightly in the wind. In the
center of the banner a simple cross signified the
heart of their belief.

As crowded as the square was, with fifty
thousand or more in attendance, all present
knew that it would be more crowded the next
day, Christmas Eve, and even more crowded
still the following day, when the Pontiff would
celebrate Christmas Day with his people.

With a white skullcap, a zucchetto, atop
his white hair, a white cape hanging nearly to
his elbows, and bright white vestments
underneath, the Pope was clearly visible on the
balcony, even to those farthest away in the sea

167

of people below. And, with such a pale
background of vestments, many could even
discern the outline of the thick golden cross that
hung from a golden chain around his neck.
Only the few attending priests on the balcony,
however, could see the kind blue eyes of the
Pontiff as he prayed aloud with his hands palms
up, held out to the side at shoulder height.

Truly, this was a Pope of the people,
sharing the prayers of Advent with them,
connecting with them through his gestures,
filling them with the joyous spirit of the season
as his soft voice carried over St. Peter's Square
through the state-of-the-art loud speakers.
Many in the crowd had come to celebrate the
season, and many had come to connect with
their shepherd.

From his vantage point on the balcony,
the Pope could see the full breadth of the
enormous circle of people as they stretched
before him through the square and beyond,
awash in the magnificent light of the setting sun.
With the utmost respect and sincerity, he spoke
each word of prayer into the microphone as
though he was able to see into the eyes, and,
perhaps, into the very soul, of each person who
heard him. It did not matter that thousands of
people could get no closer than the periphery of
the square. The strength of this Pope, many
had acclaimed for years, was his ability to
connect with his flock.

The Pope could not know that the man
in gray, lurking in the shadows at the side of the

square, lost in the sea of humanity, looked on at
the Pontiff with intentions other than those of
the masses. His bushy black eyebrows covered
dark eyes, unblinking, frozen in focus on the
balcony before him, not more than one hundred
meters away.

Slowly the man slipped his hand beneath
his long gray coat, as if he were reaching for a
cigarette in his shirt pocket. It was not a
cigarette he found, however. Ever so slightly,
the coat opened and the setting sun caught the
glint of the metal object underneath.

*   *   *   *   *

Her bangs neatly combed in a straight
line above her big brown eyes, Elizabeth's face
was the target of dozens of flashing cameras as
she came down the stairs from her house,
flanked by her mother and father, followed
closely by gray-haired Father Dunne. The press
gallery was ready, the platforms across the
street were stirring, and the enormous crowd
that filled 77th Street to capacity for several
blocks in each direction was at once anxious
and expectant. Again they cheered for their
little heroine.

Barely to the bottom of the stairs,
Elizabeth looked up, stopped, and knelt

immediately. Though there was no sign yet of the apparition, Matthew, Mary, and Father Dunne followed her lead. In an instant, however, the bright light with golden rays descended slowly from the heavens and hovered in the air above the little girl. The rays of gold rotated and undulated around the periphery of the light.

With a loud, collective gasp, and then silence, the crowd acknowledged the light's presence and most of the people fell to their knees. Though a few journalists and police officers remained standing, albeit slack-jawed, the group closest to the light knelt as well.

Little Elizabeth looked directly at the intense light, smiling, moving her lips, her eyes bright. Everyone else present, however, squinted and tried hard to catch a glimpse.

After a few minutes had passed, Elizabeth's eyes narrowed and a look of concern spread across her face. She shook her head and moved her lips more vigorously, but her words were not able to be heard. She closed her eyes and bowed her head. The light rose slowly, diminishing in size and intensity, higher and higher, fading from view, until it was gone.

Suddenly, with a jerk, Elizabeth lifted her head to the sky and opened her eyes wide. She thrust her hands toward the heavens. "Kneel!" she yelled. "Danger. Kneel. You're in danger. You must kneel now."

The police officers surveyed the crowd with their eyes, but saw nothing to warrant concern. The media were confused and turned to each other with puzzled faces. A loud buzz went up from the crowd.

With even more passion and with greater volume, Elizabeth shouted once again: "Pater sancte, periculum in mora." With that, her little body began to shake and her outstretched fingers strained upward toward the heavens. "Periculum! Periculum! Kneel."

Her eyes opened wide and her body quivered uncontrollably as she fixed her gaze above her. Suddenly her body grew rigid. It stayed that way for an instant, but then, just as she closed her eyes, she went limp and fell hard to the ground.

"She's collapsed," someone yelled from the crowd.

Matthew and Mary rushed to her side.

*   *   *   *   *

A resounding reverberation of praying voices emanated from the sea of people beneath the Pope, their prayers bouncing off the buildings surrounding St. Peter's Square and ultimately reaching his ears on the balcony. He held his hands outstretched and surveyed his flock.

Without warning, the noise stopped. He heard nothing and it startled him. He turned to his attendants on the balcony, but their actions told him immediately that they still heard the crowd.

Suddenly came a single, distinct voice, loud, clear, shouting to him. He knew he had heard this voice before but he was slow to place it.

"Danger," he heard. "Periculum."

This was too peculiar and too confusing. Trying to regain his senses, he lowered his head as if in silent prayer and the crowd knew nothing different. A few of the attendants on the balcony sensed something amiss, however, and turned their undivided attention toward him.

The voice was emphatic: "You must kneel now. There is danger in delay. Periculum in mora." His mind raced, trying to make sense of what was happening. He glanced to those attending him. Did they hear that, he asked them. They responded with puzzled looks. But he knew before he even asked them that this was a voice that only he could hear. He closed his eyes and listened. Over and over it rang out with the message, the warning.

It came to him. His eyes lit up and his brows raised. He recognized it. This was the voice of the sparrow, the thunderous voice, little Elizabeth's voice. "Kneel," it said once more.

THE MIRACLES

Immediately he knelt and outstretched his hands definitively to signal those around him on the balcony to do the same at once. All obeyed.

At that precise instant, a loud "pop" rang out from the crowd below, and then another. A split second after the first "pop" the window of the door behind the Pope shattered, and glass shards splashed to the balcony behind him.

The attendants were startled. They stayed low, hidden by, but not protected by, the banner that hung from the balcony, and they converged on the Pontiff to shelter him. Quickly, on their haunches, they ushered the Pope back through the door to safety.

There was much movement on the right side of the square about one hundred meters away. Above the commotion rose a small gray puff of smoke.

*   *   *   *   *

Seated at the bottom of the stairs outside of her house, Elizabeth smiled at her mother and father who hovered over her. She could see Father Dunne behind them. All wore concerned looks.

173

"Are you all right, sweetie?" Matthew asked.

"I'm fine, Daddy." Her big brown eyes seemed a bit glassy.

"You fainted," Mary said.

The six-year-old shook her head. "I'm fine now."

"We should take her inside," Mary said.

"Not yet, Mommy. I have to deliver Our Lady's message."

Matthew looked carefully at her eyes. "Are you sure you're okay?"

"Yes, Daddy. Please, believe me. It won't take long."

Matthew hesitated, looked at Mary, and then put his arm under Elizabeth's to help her up. "Okay. But as soon as you're finished with the message, we've got to get you inside. No answering reporters' questions today."

He led her to the table with the cluster of microphones and the media quieted down quickly. As word filtered through the crowd that the little girl was about to speak, it, too, grew silent.

Elizabeth, her bangs a bit disheveled from the fall, not quite as even across her forehead as they had been, leaned toward the microphones. "Our Lady repeated her message this morning. And she wants you to know that she will give the world a sign today, a sign that will make it clear that she has been here."

Her voice was weak, but the public address system boomed it out to the huge crowd. "Our Lady said that the whole world will be watching when the sign is given. It's important that the whole world hear her message. She repeated it over and over to me: We need to pray -- now. We shouldn't wait. We should pray to her and to her son, Jesus. They love us and they will listen."

She paused, clearing her mind, trying to determine if there was anything else to say. She looked over her shoulder at her father, standing behind her. "I think that's all, Daddy."

"Okay, sweetie," he said, scooping her up into his arms. He leaned to the cluster of microphones. "She needs rest. She won't be able to answer questions. I'm sure you can understand."

Despite his words, the journalists barked their questions at her all at once, an indecipherable cacophony of voices. That they wanted the details was clear, but their words got tangled and garbled amongst themselves.

At one point, however, several reporters did seem to have the same question, and as Matthew began to take Elizabeth toward the house, he was able to discern "What time will the sign come?"

Matthew looked at his daughter. "Do you know the time for the sign?"

"Three o'clock," she said.

Already climbing the stairs to the house, Matthew turned and said loudly "three o'clock." He turned back again and carried Elizabeth inside.

Edward F. Droge, Jr.

CHAPTER TWENTY-SEVEN

DAY SIX (Continued)

With Mary and Matthew standing beside her, Elizabeth stood by the sofa and spoke into the phone. "Thanks. I'm really glad you're safe." She paused to listen. "Okay. I think that would be fun." She paused again. "Goodbye."

She handed the phone to her mother. "He wants to talk with you."

Mary took the receiver. "Hello, Your Holiness." She paused. "Yes, someone from your office, Father Giovanni, gave us all the details this morning. We called as soon as Elizabeth explained what happened." Again she paused. "Yes, she's fine. We think it was just the tension of the moment. And we've heard that you're fine, too, and we're all so grateful."

176

THE MIRACLES

She winked at Elizabeth as she listened. "Yes, Your Holiness, Father Giovanni told us that he'll call us in advance the next time you're able to stop in New York so that we can meet with you at the airport." She smiled. "I know. I heard her say that she thinks it would be fun to see you." She listened. "Thank you, Your Holiness. Thank you." She hung up.

Matthew noticed the tears in her eyes and put his arm around her. "What's the matter?" he asked.

"He's such a good and gentle man. I'm so glad he's all right."

Elizabeth moved closer. "Me, too, Mommy."

Matthew lifted his daughter so that they could share a family hug. They stood there, the three of them, hugging silently in their living room, under the stern and watchful eye of the angel atop the Christmas tree.

CHAPTER TWENTY-EIGHT

DAY SIX (Continued)

The line filed past Elizabeth as she stood with her father at the base of the stairs in front of the house. She smiled and made a point of making eye contact with every person. They smiled back as they walked and many called to her to pray for them. She nodded assurance that she would.

The line filtered out from the enormous crowd of onlookers that jammed every inch of 77th Street. Orchestrated by police officers who funneled the people between stanchions that lined the sidewalk, the line proceeded from an area near the tenements on the 5th Avenue side of the Depaul home, past the house, and into an area on the 6th Avenue side.

THE MIRACLES

As one particular woman passed, she broke slowly, methodically from the line and stepped toward the police officers standing near the stanchions set up to separate Elizabeth from the crowd. Two police officers reacted quickly and stepped directly in her way. She seemed no threat except that she had violated forbidden space.

The woman was wearing a dark coat and had a dark kerchief on her head. "I just want to thank you," she shouted to Elizabeth.

The little girl turned her full attention in her direction.

The woman stopped at the stanchion and was barely able to see Elizabeth between the two police officers. "You spoke to my mother at church," she shouted.

Elizabeth wore a puzzled face and looked up to her father. He shrugged his shoulders, signifying that he did not know what she was talking about.

"My name is Agnes Yuroslavak," she shouted. "I was in the hospital and you prayed with my mother that I would get well."

Elizabeth's eyes lit up. "I remember, Daddy," she said, looking up to him. "The woman who came up to us when we went to see Father Dunne at church. She and I prayed for her daughter Agnes."

Matthew's expression said that he, too, remembered now. "Father Dunne said she had a brain tumor and was dying."

"Thank you," shouted the woman.
"Thank you."

The police officers told her to move along and she obeyed. As she did, however, Elizabeth smiled widely at her.

"I remember," Elizabeth shouted to her. "You were healed because of your faith, because you believed."

Filling with tears, the woman's eyes fixed on the little girl's and expressed her gratitude without the need for further words. She continued to walk away slowly, her gaze still locked on Elizabeth, and the soulful look on her face carved a profound and durable impression into the mind of the six-year-old.

Elizabeth felt a chill go up her spine with the renewed acknowledgement of the power of prayer. To herself, she thanked Jesus for making one of his people whole again, and she thanked the Blessed Virgin for interceding for her with her Son.

Matthew looked at his watch and seeing him do it prompted Elizabeth to ask for the time.

"It's just three o'clock," he said.

Elizabeth looked up. White, wispy clouds fanned out like cotton across the bright blue sky. She relished the warmth of the sun. Truly it was a perfect day for Our Lady's sign.

She looked toward the platform and saw the activity, like bees in a hive, reporters and tech crew bustling about, brushing each other in close quarters. In the assembly of media in

front of her, many reporters, too, were checking
their watches and surveying the sky.

What would the sign be, Elizabeth
wondered. What would the Blessed Virgin do
to capture the world's attention?

Her mother had told her that at Fatima,
Portugal in 1917, Our Lady had appeared to
three children, and at that time, too, she had
given the world a sign. Thousands of people
reported back then that they had witnessed the
sun dancing in the sky.

Would the sun dance today, Elizabeth
wondered.

Several minutes passed and it was
increasingly clear that the media and the crowd
were aware of the time. But no sign was
visible.

Ten more minutes passed, and then
twenty. The sky was clear. Many in the crowd
seemed impatient, shouting out "Where is the
sign?" and imploring Elizabeth to "Do
something," as if the little six-year-old had
control over the situation.

"Maybe the sign isn't supposed to be in
the sky, Daddy," Elizabeth said.

Matthew nodded. "That's very
possible." He looked at his watch again. "The
Blessed Virgin didn't say specifically that it
would be in the sky, did she?"

"She didn't say at all what it would be.
Only that all the world would be watching and
would know that it was a sign from her, to
show that she was appearing here."

"We have to be patient then," Matthew said. "We have to trust in Our Lady."

Elizabeth continued to smile at the passersby in the line but she could not help noticing the heightened activity on the television platforms and the increased uneasiness of the crowd.

Matthew, too, was calm and confident on the outside, but aware of the building tension with each passing minute. He could see the faces of the reporters in the media assembly grow restless. Randall Prens, in particular, looked impatient and, it seemed to Matthew, he was spreading his impatience to the others around him.

*   *   *   *   *

Head down, wearing her yellow sleeper pajamas, Elizabeth sat near the Christmas tree with her back against the staircase. Mechanically, she stroked the black and white fur of Fluffy, the stuffed cat that lay faithfully at her side.

She lifted her big brown eyes to gaze at the Christmas tree. Maybe that would cheer her up, she thought. The colored lights and ornaments dressed the tree from head to toe, and the modest measure of tinsel added a touch of glimmer.

182

THE MIRACLES

Her eyes met the eyes of the angel glaring down from the top. His wings spread wide, his arms outstretched, he seemed to be looking directly at her.

"Why didn't the Blessed Virgin's sign appear?" she wondered, half hoping that the angel would be able to hear the question and answer it for her. It was clear that many people had been disappointed when there was no sign at three o'clock...or four o'clock...no sign at all, even now.

She looked toward the kitchen to check the time. Her mother was rinsing off the dinner dishes. The clock said it was ten after six. And still no sign.

In her mind, she reviewed the awkward moments outside. Of course, she, herself, was crushed that the sign had not come, but she knew from the reaction of the crowd that many others were crushed, too. They had trusted her word. They had fully expected to see the sign today. They believed; they trusted; and they were disappointed.

She knew, too, that many in the crowd who had come to 77th Street because they did *not* believe and did *not* trust, who had wanted or needed to see with their own eyes this miracle that they had heard about, were disappointed as well, but, more important, were also given ammunition for their distrust and their inevitable criticism.

She knew the crowd had held non-believers. Even if she had not heard the jeers, it was understandable that not all present, not all of the tens of thousands present, were ready to accept blindly the word of a six-year-old that the Blessed Virgin, the Queen of Heaven, the Mother of Jesus was appearing on an obscure street in Brooklyn, delivering a message of the greatest importance to the entire world, and trusting it with this little girl.

No, it was too much to accept without a sign of some sort. Our Lady knew this, Elizabeth thought. It was extremely important for the world to receive a sign that would confirm Our Lady's appearances, that would prompt people of all faiths to listen to the message, to the call for prayer and conversion.

She picked up the stuffed cat and cradled it in her arms. At least Fluffy was still there for her, she thought. She knew she was going to have to be strong. The Blessed Virgin had told her that it would be difficult. Trust in her, Our Lady had said.

Elizabeth glanced at the television. Her father had left it on when he went upstairs for something. The volume was too low for her to hear but she saw the woman newscaster with the box over her shoulder. In the box was a picture of the Pope. Elizabeth smiled. At least something good happened today. She knew that the newscaster was reporting the story of the shooting.

The video image in the box over the woman's shoulder changed to a sweeping view of the enormous crowd that had been on 77th

184

Street earlier in the day. When the image changed again, Elizabeth saw herself in the box, first kneeling, praying, and then sitting at the table, speaking into the microphones. She knew what the woman newscaster must have been saying. She knew that she was telling the story of the sign that never came.

The image in the box changed again, this time to a view of the blue sky above 77th Street. Except for a few wispy clouds that looked like cotton, it was empty.

A tear fell from Elizabeth's eye to Fluffy's fur.

CHAPTER TWENTY-NINE

DAY SIX (Continued)

Matthew sat on the sofa and admired the Christmas tree. The television was on but he preferred to place most of his attention on the tree at this hour. He listened half heartedly to the all-news channel, but he had heard it all already anyway. There was only so much he cared to hear about the profile of the person who had shot at the Pope. And there was nothing more that he cared to hear about the sign that never came to 77th Street.

He sat up straighter when he heard a sound coming from the rear of the house. It sounded like a knocking on the back door. He grabbed the remote control to mute the television just as the male news anchor said:

THE MIRACLES

"Coming up next, a chilling story out of Hawaii that you'll find hard to believe..."

Matthew walked slowly toward the back door. He looked at his watch. It was after nine. Who would be knocking at the back door at this hour?

As he approached the door, he could see a figure outside, but it was too dark to tell whether it was a man or a woman. He flicked on the light switch as he opened the door and saw the thick blonde hair of Randall Prens.

"Mr. Prens!"

"Hello, Mr. Depaul. I'm terribly sorry for visiting like this -- coming to your back door at this hour -- but we're running a story tomorrow and I thought it very important that I speak to you first. I couldn't get through on the phone."

"Come in."

Matthew led him to the living room and motioned him to the sofa. "Can I get you anything," Matthew said, "a cup of coffee or something?"

Prens waved his hand. "No. Thanks. I'm fine."

Mary came down the stairs. "I thought I heard someone come in," she said.

Prens stood.

"Hello, Mr. Prens. To what do we owe the pleasure?"

"I was telling your husband. We're running a story tomorrow and I wanted to give

187

you a chance to add to it, if you want." He sat down again and Mary sat next to her husband.

"A story about what?" Matthew asked.

"About the alleged apparitions..."

Matthew noted the word "alleged" again and remembered that Prens had used it emphatically at one of the briefings outside, indicating a clear distrust.

The reporter continued. "...Let me be direct. I've been in contact with several people in researching this story, including a Mr. Tom Porter at Lexington Laser Works. Have you ever heard of the company?"

Both Matthew and Mary shook their heads to indicate that they had not.

"Well, anyhow, Tom Porter had read the coverage of the alleged apparitions and called me yesterday to tell me that he could produce a light similar to the one that was described in the newspaper as having appeared in front of your house."

Matthew sensed what was coming, but let the reporter speak uninterrupted.

"I went to Lexington Laser Works," Prens said, "and, sure enough, Tom Porter was able to produce a similar light, although it didn't have the golden rays coming from it. It hovered in the air quite remarkably. He tried to explain the technology to me, something about lasers and holograms, but, frankly, I just wasn't able to understand much of what he was saying. I really didn't have to. Having seen the light, itself, was enough."

THE MIRACLES

Matthew did not want to make any assumptions about what Prens was saying. "What exactly are you getting at?" Matthew said.

"What I'm getting at is that there are alternative explanations to the source of the light that has been appearing in front of your house. I've seen a similar light that was man-made, and it did not hold the Mother of Jesus, as your daughter has claimed the other light contained."

Mary took affront. "Are you saying that our daughter is lying, Mr. Prens?"

The reporter shook his head. "I'm saying only that we have no proof one way or another. We can't see the woman that your daughter describes. We see only the light. And, now, after today's disappointment with the sign that was promised but..."

Matthew leaned forward toward Prens and interrupted. "Let me be sure I understand you. You're saying that we could be producing the light somehow and using our six-year-old child to perpetrate some grand hoax about the appearance of the Blessed Virgin?"

"I'm saying that there are alternatives -- yes, that's one of them. My story in tomorrow's paper will present alternative explanations. The readers will be left to make their own judgments."

Mary had heard enough. She stood. "You have some nerve, Mr. Prens, coming into our house and making accusations like this."

"I wanted to give you a chance to defend your position."

Now Matthew stood. "We don't feel as if we have to defend ourselves, Mr. Prens. We haven't asked for any attention. In fact, in the beginning, you'll recall, we tried to avoid attention."

Prens stood now.

Matthew continued. "There's nothing we can do to stop you from writing your story, but that's all it is, a story. You know better -- I'm sure of that -- but for some reason, you think it's important to try to refute what you know is true. I feel sorry for you, Mr. Prens."

Matthew's face was turning red. "I think you should leave now. There's nothing else to say."

Prens did not try to say anything further. He walked slowly to the back door, and went out.

Mary's attention was drawn to the top of the stairs. There, sitting on the top step in her sleepers, Elizabeth held Fluffy in her arms. Apparently, the little girl had heard the conversation, for Mary could see the tears streaming down her daughter's face. She rushed up the stairs to comfort her.

CHAPTER THIRTY

DAY SEVEN -- CHRISTMAS EVE

Matthew measured the coffee carefully, spoonful by spoonful, and put them one-by-one into the filter. His mind wandered to the conversation with Prens the previous night.

He shook his head with disappointment, not so much for the distrust of the reporter, but for the influence that the story might have on some of those who read it. Some, Matthew knew, would be discouraged from believing that the Blessed Virgin, in fact, had appeared, and her message in those cases would fall on deaf ears

He padded to the door. As much as he dreaded it, he knew he had to read the story. He opened the door and was surprised at what he saw. A thin layer of snow covered 77th

191

Street and heavy flakes were streaming through the lights of the streetlamps.

Aside from two police officers leaning against the stanchions at the bottom of the stairs, and a handful of the faithful onlookers lingering in the road, 77th Street was ghostly desolate. The platforms in front of Mrs. Mulrooney's house were empty and devoid of activity for the first time in days.

Christmas Eve, Matthew thought. They wanted to be with their families on Christmas Eve. Deep down, though, he knew the more obvious reason. There had been no sign, as promised yesterday. It had not taken much for the masses to lose faith.

But, then, he thought, it was early. Maybe the crowd would return. Maybe it would not be as large as it had been, but he could hope that the crowd would return. Our Lady wanted her message heard. He was left to wonder what kind of a crowd would have been standing before him at this moment had the sign appeared yesterday.

He retrieved the newspaper, nodded to the police officers, and returned to the warmth of the house. He threw the paper on the table and poured himself a cup of coffee.

As he sat, he could see the headline: "Doubts Raised About Apparitions." In smaller letters underneath: "No Sign; Thousands Disappointed." And in even smaller letters underneath that: "Alternative Explanations

Posited for Phenomenon." And, finally, the byline: "by Randall Prens."

Matthew read the story and was not surprised. It was as Prens had said it would be. Matthew shook his head without realizing it. Prens had gone out of his way to debunk the apparitions and Matthew found it difficult to accept.

Having read enough, he threw the paper back on the table. Another headline, however, caught his eye: "Snowstorm Hits Hawaii." Matthew's eyes opened a bit wider. Snow in Hawaii? He recalled the television newscaster mentioning a story about Hawaii just as Prens knocked last night. Matthew had turned it off without hearing about the snow.

How unusual, Matthew thought. He had never heard of snow in Hawaii. He read the story and, sure enough, it confirmed that this was the first recorded snowstorm known to hit the islands in the Pacific. Even odder, the writer pointed out, was the fact that it had come from nowhere. No one had been able to predict it. The sky had been clear one minute and, suddenly, filled with clouds the next.

Meteorologists said it "defied the laws of Nature" in a zone where the winter temperatures were generally in the 60's. There was no rational explanation for snow clouds suddenly appearing. Scientists were calling it "extraordinary," "extremely unusual," "absolutely baffling."

The phrase "Man bites dog" flashed into Matthew's head. Editors wanted stories out of the ordinary. Not "dog bites man," but "man bites dog." This was the kind of story that the media dreams about, the kind that reverses the routine, the commonplace, the kind that has enough appeal to capture the world's attention. This was big news.

Matthew's jaw dropped. Wait a minute. Could it be? He had just said it himself -- this was the kind of story that captured the world's attention. Was this the work of the Blessed Virgin?

He took a sip of his coffee and tossed the thoughts around in his head. Our Lady had said that the whole world would be watching. Well, surely, the whole world would be watching a story about snow in Hawaii.

But it did not quite fit. Our Lady had said also that the sign would make it clear that she had appeared here on 77th Street. How would anyone, Matthew wondered, be able to make a connection between the snow in Hawaii and the apparitions in Brooklyn?

Nevertheless, he was taken by the notion. He put down his coffee cup and scampered up the stairs.

Mary was sleeping peacefully when he entered the bedroom. He could not keep this to himself a minute longer. He sat on the bed and bent over to kiss her on the cheek. She smiled and slowly rolled over.

"It's snowing in Hawaii," he said.

THE MIRACLES

"What?" She wondered if she were dreaming.

"There's a story in the paper -- on the front page. It's actually snowing in Hawaii. Rush hour traffic in Honolulu was at a complete standstill for hours."

She sat up. She was not sure what to make of this. "Well, okay."

"Don't you find that unusual?"

She still had not shaken the cobwebs completely from her head. "Yes," she said slowly. "Yes, snow in Hawaii is very unusual."

"Right. And do you think it's just a coincidence that it snows in Hawaii on the day that Our Lady told Elizabeth the world would be given a sign?"

Mary sat up straighter now. She put her hand over her mouth in surprise. She understood the connection. "Oh, my goodness!"

Matthew stood and started out of the room. "I'll pour you a cup of coffee," he said.

Mary jumped out of bed, put on her white flannel robe, and followed her husband downstairs. As he attended to the coffee, she read the article.

He placed a steaming cup in front of her. "It's too much of a coincidence," he said, "for it not to be related."

She put down the paper to look him in the eye. "Did you read the whole story?" she asked.

"No."

"Read this." She pushed the paper toward him and pointed at a particular paragraph. She jumped up and ran to the bookcase in the living room.

He read it aloud as she returned to the table with an atlas. "It started at ten o'clock and by the afternoon rush hour, traffic was delayed for hours." He looked at her. "Why is that important?"

She rustled through the pages of the book in front of her and when she found what she was looking for, she pushed the book in front of her husband. It was a map of the United States, showing the time zones at the top of the page.

He smiled when he realized what she was pointing out. "The snow started at ten yesterday morning," he said, "which is three o'clock in the afternoon in New York."

"Our Lady did give the world a sign at three o'clock," Mary said. "We just didn't know it. We assumed that it would be here."

Matthew took a deep breath. "But how will people know that this is really the sign? You can bet that Prens and a lot of others will see it as coincidence, unconnected."

Mary reviewed it for a moment and then sighed. Matthew was probably right, she thought.

They heard a creaking sound and turned toward it. Elizabeth, rubbing her eyes with one hand, holding Fluffy with the other, was walking tentatively down the stairs. She was wearing her sleepers.

"Good morning, sweetie," Mary said.

Elizabeth joined them at the kitchen table.

"We've got some news," said Matthew.

*   *   *   *   *

Early morning traffic on Highway 1 in Honolulu was at a crawl as snow continued to fall. A white blanket lay over the road. Nearly one day into this bizarre storm and the clouds gave no hint of relenting.

Motorists, not accustomed to such slippery roads, inched along to avoid accidents. Through virtually every windshield, anger and frustration were apparent.

Suddenly, though, as quickly as it had started, the snow stopped. The clouds began to part. The blue of the sky was returning. People ran into the streets. Motorists jumped from their cars. Cheers could be heard from every quarter of the capital city and beyond.

Farther and farther apart, the clouds travelled. The sky grew brighter and brighter.

Without warning, the blue of the sky turned to red, as red as the petal of a rose. Then, a moment later, the red turned to golden

yellow, a glimmering, glistening, golden yellow,
that made the heavens seem an endless,
seamless sheet of precious metal.
    Wide-eyed and slack-jawed, the people
on these enchanted islands stared at the
alternating colors of the sky. From blue to red
to golden yellow, the canvas above them
changed before their very eyes, radiating its
hues upon them and filling them with awe.
    At once, an enormous ball of flames of
orange and red filled the heavens. Beside the
ball came a vision, a huge and daunting angel, a
transparent, three dimensional figure of strength
and power. With armor across his massive
chest, and with a sword at his side, this
fearsome creature dwarfed the glowing, flaming
ball beside him.
    Many below were frozen in their place,
unable to move, watching in shock. Others ran
in horror, yelling and shouting and screaming.
But their screams of terror and panic were
drowned by a tremendous thunder from the sky,
a rumbling, rolling thunder that had no mercy
on their ears.
    The angel drew his sword and held it
high, and, with that motion, the thunder roared
more loudly. Streams of flames spewed from
the fiery ball.
    Abruptly, the thunder stopped and an
eerie silence reigned. But in a moment a choir
of angelic voices resounded in the heavens,
singing glory and praise to God. From the ball,
fire burned in different directions across the sky,

until, after only a few seconds, an enormous, blazing outline appeared.

It was a bird. A sparrow. An enormous flaming outline of a sparrow, its wings flapping, stretching across the heavens, wide enough to be clearly visible for miles and miles. In the sparrow's mouth, a flaming black rosary dangled. A silver tag that said "Elizabeth" contrasted with the blackness of the beads.

Every camera in Honolulu and the surrounding area shot skyward and captured the moment. Gasps and screams emerged from those who witnessed it. Many people fainted.

*   *   *   *   *

Snow fell lazily on to 77th Street. The setting sun cast a russet mantle on the sky.

From speakers above the front door of Mrs. Mulrooney's house, a choir sang a hymn of glory and praise that filled the frosty air and penetrated the living rooms of the surrounding houses.

Matthew, Mary, and Elizabeth stood by their Christmas tree, hugging. Fluffy lay on the floor nearby.

The light from the television danced into the room as the screen filled with the images of

the flaming sparrow and black rosary, set
against the golden sky of Honolulu.

Above the Depauls, at the very top of
the tree, the stern-faced angel symbolically cast
its sphere of protection upon them with wide
wings and outstretched arms.

Elizabeth looked up and smiled. For
just an instant, and only for her to see, the angel
smiled back.

NOTE

It is no coincidence that you have read this book. You were meant to read it. "You have not chosen me; I have chosen you. Go and bear fruit that will last." (John 15:16)

If the story has touched you, please let us know. (Use address below for author or publisher.)

If you would like to provide copies for your church, school, or other organizations, please inquire about the special distribution program.

Address all correspondence to:
Droge, P.O. Box 205, Greenwich, NY 12834

ABOUT THE GENESIS OF THIS BOOK

Edward F. Droge, Jr. is quick to acknowledge the divine inspiration that resulted in this book, but he refrains from revealing the details. "I can tell you only that it began," he says, "when something sacred, amazing, mysterious, and inexplicable happened to me in a visit to France in 1972. I returned to the U.S. thinking I might never understand it. More than 20 years later, however, in a very special and personal moment, I was 'given' the explanation, and, at the same time, I was 'given' the story of THE MIRACLES." In an act of faith, he committed himself to turning the story into a book, and, as he worked, he continued to "receive" the words written on these pages. He will not make known who "gave" him the story but does say, "Readers of THE MIRACLES will know."